"So…what should I tell him?" Mitch prompted.

"That I'm not interested in dating anyone right now and, even if I was, I'd never go out with the guy who threw my favorite Beanie Baby into a tree at Prospect Park."

"I forgot that was Austin," he said.

"Well, I didn't," Lindsay assured him. "And I didn't forget who climbed the tree to get it back for me, either." She reached out then to trace her fingertip along the jagged three-inch scar on the inside of his forearm—courtesy of the branch that broke when he was in the tree, hastening his descent and gouging the flesh.

"You cried when you saw the blood," he said, wanting—needing—to focus on something other than the way his blood heated in response to her gentle touch.

She lifted her gaze to his then, her eyes twinkling with humor. "I cried because you got blood on my Beanie Baby."

"I did not," he denied. "I tossed it down to you from the tree."

"My hero," she said lightly.

"I'm nobody's hero," he assured her.

"You're mine," she insisted. "For a lot more reasons than rescuing Beanie Babies."

Dear Reader,

The sun is shining, birds are chirping and flowers are blooming—all signs that spring is in the air.

After a long, cold winter, I'm always happy to put away the bulky coats and heavy boots, eager to go outside and feel the warmth of the sun on my face and breathe in the fragrance of fresh cut grass. (Apologies to those who suffer seasonal allergies, but it's one of my favorite scents this time of year!)

Spring has long been celebrated as a season of awakening and renewal, as Lindsay Thomas is about to discover... The single mom's heart went into hibernation after the death of her husband more than two years earlier, and then it was roused by an unexpected New Year's Eve kiss from Mitchell Gilmore.

Lindsay and Mitchell have been friends for a long time, and both are wary about changing the nature of their relationship. But as winter gives way to spring—and with the help of Lindsay's two adorable children—that longtime camaraderie just might begin to blossom into something more...

I hope you enjoy this return to Haven, Nevada, and Lindsay and Mitchell's story.

Happy reading!

Brenda Harlen

PS: For up to date information on my new releases (or to discover my backlist titles), check out my website, brendaharlen.com, or follow me on Facebook.

The Rancher's Promise

BRENDA HARLEN

HARLEQUIN
SPECIAL
EDITION

HARLEQUIN®
SPECIAL EDITION™

ISBN-13: 978-1-335-40479-4

The Rancher's Promise

Copyright © 2021 by Brenda Harlen

All rights reserved. No part of this book may be used or reproduced in
any manner whatsoever without written permission except in the case of
brief quotations embodied in critical articles and reviews.

This is a work of fiction. Names, characters, places and incidents
are either the product of the author's imagination or are used fictitiously.
Any resemblance to actual persons, living or dead, businesses,
companies, events or locales is entirely coincidental.

This edition published by arrangement with Harlequin Books S.A.

For questions and comments about the quality of this book,
please contact us at CustomerService@Harlequin.com.

Harlequin Enterprises ULC
22 Adelaide St. West, 40th Floor
Toronto, Ontario M5H 4E3, Canada
www.Harlequin.com

Printed in U.S.A.

Recycling programs
for this product may
not exist in your area.

PLEASE RECYCLE · THIS PRODUCT IS RECYCLABLE

Brenda Harlen is a former attorney who once had the privilege of appearing before the Supreme Court of Canada. The practice of law taught her a lot about the world and reinforced her determination to become a writer—because in fiction, she could promise a happy ending! Now she is an award-winning, RITA® Award–nominated nationally bestselling author of more than thirty titles for Harlequin. You can keep up-to-date with Brenda on Facebook and Twitter, or through her website, brendaharlen.com.

Books by Brenda Harlen

Harlequin Special Edition

Match Made in Haven

Claiming the Cowboy's Heart
Double Duty for the Cowboy
One Night with the Cowboy
A Chance for the Rancher
The Marine's Road Home
Meet Me Under the Mistletoe

Montana Mavericks: What Happened to Beatrix?

A Cowboy's Christmas Carol

Montana Mavericks: Six Brides for Six Brothers

Maverick Christmas Surprise

Montana Mavericks: The Lonelyhearts Ranch

Bring Me a Maverick for Christmas!

Visit the Author Profile page
at Harlequin.com for more titles.

For Susan Litman, who has been with me from the beginning, helping to make every one of my stories better—and reminding me to breathe when I forget. Thank you for everything!

Prologue

Lindsay Delgado was ten years old when Mitchell Gilmore asked her to marry him.

She accepted his proposal because they were friends, and she figured that if she had to marry someone, it should be someone she actually *liked*. Then he gave her a plastic ring with a purple flower on it that he got for twenty-five cents out of a vending machine at Jo's Pizza, and they sealed their deal with a kiss.

It was her first proposal and her first kiss.

Now, fifteen years later, it was finally her wedding day.

And though she was wearing a sparkling diamond on her finger now, she still had that plastic token, usually tucked in the secret bottom compartment of her jewelry box.

Sentimental nonsense, her great-aunt Edna would say.

And maybe she was right.

But Lindsay didn't care, because she'd always love the boy who'd given it to her.

She turned to face the mirror and brushed her hands over the tulle skirt of her off-the-shoulder wedding gown. Saying yes to her soon-to-be-husband's proposal had been a lot easier than saying yes to the dress, and she must have tried on a hundred different styles before deciding the simple ball gown with lace at the hem was "the one." She'd originally dismissed the suggestion of a veil—until her mom had offered the one she'd worn at her own wedding and then carefully packed away in the hope that she might have a daughter who wanted to wear it one day.

"It can be your something old and something borrowed," Marilyn Delgado said. (Apparently, Lindsay got her sentimentality from her mother's side of the family.)

She'd nodded, unwilling to confess that she already had something old: the purple plastic flower ring that she'd secured to the hem of her skirt with a few loops of thread.

"Are you ready?" her sister asked now, offering the arrangement of garden roses, ranunculus, hellebores, freesia and gardenias to the bride.

Lindsay accepted the flowers as a brisk knock sounded on the door and then her father stepped into the room.

It was time.

A kaleidoscope of butterflies took flight in her tummy, swirling and twirling.

"Lindsay…oh my." His moss-green eyes—a dreamy shade inherited by each of his daughters—grew misty. "Look at you…you look like a princess bride."

"Thanks, Dad." And though she didn't think she'd ever seen a more handsome hero on the cover of any romance novel than Jackson Delgado in his classic black tuxedo with a gardenia boutonniere pinned to his lapel, the sudden tightness of her throat prevented her from expressing the thought aloud.

Behind her, Kristyne cleared her own throat. Loudly.

Their father's lips curved in an indulgent smile as his gaze shifted to his younger daughter.

Lindsay smiled, too, grateful to her sister for defusing the emotional powder keg moment so that she wouldn't walk down the aisle with mascara smeared under her eyes.

"Yes, I see you, too, Kristyne," Jackson assured her.

"Just checking," the taffeta-clad maid of honor said with a dramatic sniff.

"And you look almost as beautiful as the bride," their father noted.

"I can't wait until I *am* the bride," Kristyne said, perhaps a little wistfully. "Of course, Gabe has to propose first."

"Don't be in such a hurry," Jackson admonished. "You're young yet."

"Are you saying that I'm old?" Lindsay couldn't resist teasing him.

"I'm saying that your groom is growing old, waiting for the two of you to stop yakking so we can get this show on the road," he said, deftly sidestepping the loaded question.

"Well, let's not make him wait any longer," the bride said.

Kristyne grabbed her own flowers, then brushed a quick kiss on her sister's cheek. "Love you."

"Love you, too," Lindsay managed, though her throat had tightened up again.

As the maid of honor headed out of the room, Jackson bent his arm, and Lindsay tucked her hand into the crook of his elbow.

The organist was playing Pachelbel's "Canon in D" and Kristyne waited for her cue, then began to make her way down the aisle.

"You're trembling," Jackson murmured softly, looking at his daughter with concern.

"I'm a little nervous," she admitted.

"Are you ready to do this? Because if you're having second thoughts, we can turn around and walk right out that door over there," he said.

He'd let her do it, too.

Lindsay had no doubt about that.

Over the past several months, her dad had grumbled—mostly good-naturedly—about what this wedding was costing him, but if she told him that she wasn't one hundred percent certain she was doing the right thing, he would tell her to wait until she was. Because marriage was forever and when she made her vows, she needed to feel confident in every word.

From this day forward...till death do us part.

"Linds?" he prompted.

"I'm ready," she said, hoping she sounded more confident than she felt as the organist transitioned to Wagner's "Bridal Chorus."

She drew a deep breath and peeked around the

corner, looking toward the front of the church. She caught Mitchell's eye and, when he winked at her, the butterflies in her tummy immediately settled.

Then she walked down the aisle to marry his best friend.

Chapter One

"I don't know why I ever agreed to go to this stupid party," Lindsay muttered, staring at the clothes strewn all over the floor of her bedroom.

But she did know.

She'd been goaded into it by her sister, who'd argued that nothing said "grieving widow" more clearly than staying home and eating a tub of ice cream by oneself on New Year's Eve.

Of course, Lindsay *was* a widow and, in her mind, entitled to indulge her penchant for frozen deliciousness every now and again. (And sometimes more frequently.)

Except that was what she'd done the previous New

Year's Eve. And the one before that. And even she had to admit that three years in a row might push her beyond "grieving" to "pitiful," and what kind of example would that set for her children?

So when her oldest and dearest friend told her that he had an extra ticket for the "Cheer for the New Year" party at Diggers' Bar & Grill and asked if she wanted to go, she'd impulsively said yes. She could have used her kids as an excuse to decline, but she knew that Suzanne and Arthur Thomas, always happy to spend time with their grandchildren, would be overjoyed to keep Elliott and Avenlea for the night.

And they were. In fact, they didn't even ask why their daughter-in-law needed someone to watch the kids. Of course, she'd told them anyway, wanting to ensure that they knew she wasn't going on a date but just spending a few hours out with Mitchell Gilmore.

"Have a good time," her mother-in-law said, practically shoving Lindsay out the door after she'd exchanged hugs and kisses with her son and daughter.

"Happy New Year," her father-in-law added with a wave.

"You, too," Lindsay said. "And thanks again."

But she was talking to the door.

As she drove the short distance from her in-laws' house to her own, she tried to muster some enthusiasm for the night ahead.

She had no doubt that Elliott and Avenlea would have a great time with Gramma and Grampa T—as they were known to distinguish them from her own parents, Gramma and Grampa D. The Thomases were wonderful grandparents who always planned activities to entertain and engage them. In fact, the presence of both sets of grandparents in Haven had been a major factor in Lindsay's decision to move back to her hometown after her husband's funeral.

Losing Nathan in a small plane crash on his way home from a business trip had been a shock. The suddenness and unexpectedness of it had made Lindsay wonder and worry about what might happen to Elliott and Avenlea if they stayed in Moose Creek and something happened to her. Sure, she and Nathan had made friends in the almost six years that they'd lived in Alaska—good friends, even—but she wanted to be near family.

And then, barely eleven months after she'd brought her children home to Haven, her parents had moved to a warmer climate for their retirement. Actually, they'd made the decision to move two years prior to that, after a particularly harsh winter that had taken a toll on Marilyn's arthritic joints. Then they got the call from Lindsay, telling them that Nathan was dead.

So Marilyn and Jackson had put their plans on hold to be in Haven when their eldest daughter came home, to offer her support and comfort and much needed help with her preschool-aged son and infant daughter. But even in the midst of her paralyzing grief and mind-numbing exhaustion, Lindsay could see that her mom struggled through the cold weather months. When she summoned the courage to ask if they'd ever considered moving south, they admitted that they'd already bought a condo in a retirement community in Arizona. They were just waiting for Lindsay and Elliott and Avenlea to be settled before they called the real estate agent to put a sign on the front lawn.

The decision to buy her parents' house had been an easy one for Lindsay. She had so many happy memories from her own childhood at 355 Winterberry Drive that she was pleased by the prospect of raising her own kids there. When Kristyne learned that her sister was buying it, she'd threatened to start a bidding war, but Lindsay knew she was only teasing. In fact, Kristyne and her husband, Gabe, had already bought a house of their own on Sagebrush Lane, only a few blocks away.

As Lindsay had passed their street on her way home, she'd considered FaceTiming her sister for help figuring out what to wear to the party. But she'd resisted, because she was trying really hard to stand on her own two feet, to prove to her friends and family that she could. That more than two years—actually two years, three months and seventeen days—after her husband's sudden death, she was finally moving on with her life.

If only she actually believed it was true.

Because staring at the entire contents of her wardrobe, haphazardly strewn over her bed and across the floor, she started to cry. Tears of grief and frustration and anger, because yes, it had been twenty-seven months and seventeen days, and she was still mad at her husband for leaving her. And yes, she knew it was completely irrational and patently unreasonable to blame him for his death, but she didn't care. They'd made promises to one another and plans for their life together—so many plans that would never come to fruition now, because Nathan was gone.

...till death do us part.

She sank to the floor and hugged her knees close to her chest as her shoulders shook and tears streamed down her face.

Damn you, Nathan. How could you do this to me? How could you leave me to raise our babies alone?

Of course, their children weren't babies anymore.

Elliott was five and a half already and Avenlea would turn three in May—coincidentally the same age that Elliott had been when she'd had to tell him that his daddy was gone. It hurt Lindsay to realize that his memories of his father were fading every day, and even more so to know that her daughter didn't have any. But there was a picture in a silver frame on her dresser to ensure Avenlea knew that she'd been loved by her daddy.

In the photo, the three-month-old was sleeping contentedly in Nathan's arms. It was a candid shot that Lindsay had snapped with the camera on her phone when she happened to be walking by. Nathan had no idea that she'd paused in the doorway to capture the moment, and the picture of her husband smiling down at their baby girl with a look of unmistakable love and pride was one of her absolute favorites.

It was also one of the last photos she had of father and daughter, because he'd been killed only a few weeks later, on his way home to his family after one of his short albeit frequent business trips.

The amount of travel required for his job as a project manager at Moose Creek Mining sometimes left Lindsay feeling like a single parent, but she couldn't really complain when his income allowed her to stay at home full-time with Elliott and work toward her Masters of Library and Information Science degree. Then she'd gotten pregnant with Avenlea, and the prospect of putting her education to use seemed further away than ever. She loved being a mom and she was happy at home with her children, but being the primary—and sometimes exclusive—caregiver wasn't always easy.

They'd had a brief argument before he left for that fated trip. She couldn't even remember what it was about anymore. Something silly, no doubt. But they'd talked later that night, after he'd checked into his hotel in Anchorage, and he'd told her to forget it, assuring her that he already had. Still, she'd planned a special dinner for his return, wanting to make it up to him. Buttermilk fried chicken and roasted potatoes and creamed corn—all his favorite foods. But he'd never made it home for that meal…

Her phone chimed, jolting her back to the present.

Mitchell, she guessed, even before she glanced at the screen to read the text message.

Are you ready?

She wiped her hands over her wet cheeks and glanced around at the various and numerous outfits she'd considered and rejected for the party. And though she felt just the teensiest bit guilty for canceling at the eleventh hour, she sent her response:

I'm sorry, but I'm not going to be able to make it tonight.

The guilt weighed a little heavier when she read his immediate reply:

Are you okay? Are the kids okay?

Yeah, we're all good. They're with their grandparents. I just don't feel up to going anywhere.

It took him a little longer to respond to that, so she was surprised when the next message that came through was simply two letters:

OK

She waited for something more—an attempt to persuade or cajole or otherwise change her mind, but apparently that was all her longtime friend intended to say on the subject. So Lindsay allowed herself to breathe a sigh of relief, even as she worried that he might be mad—and justifiably so.

Her best friend since second grade, Mitchell had been there for her in more ways than she could count since she'd moved back to Haven. And in all that time, he hadn't asked anything of her other than that she attend the annual New Year's Eve party at Diggers' with him.

She wanted to go, to be there for him as he'd been

there for her, but she wasn't ready to subject herself to the stares and whispers that, even after more than two years, had yet to completely subside. She was hardly the only widow in town, but she was "so young" to be on her own—and raising "two adorable children," too. Really, it was "so tragic" that her husband had been taken in the prime of his life, and how was she doing?

Lindsay would force a smile and respond that she was doing just fine, thank you, even when it had been a blatant lie. Because admitting that she was barely holding on to the fraying end of her rope would have been uncomfortable for everyone. Only two people—Kristyne and Mitchell—had known the truth.

They were the only two people she could always be completely honest with, which was why she felt guilty about lying to Mitchell tonight. But it was for the best. Because although she was doing much better now, today was not a good day, and she knew that he would have a much better time at the party without her.

She froze when the doorbell rang and silently berated herself for assuming that his "OK" meant that he'd accepted her decision to stay home tonight. But she had no intention of letting herself be persuaded or cajoled, so she stayed right where she was, on the floor of her bedroom, waiting for him to give up and go away so that she could binge on the tub of rocky road ice cream she knew was in the freezer.

Mitch wasn't at all surprised when Lindsay bailed on their plans for the evening. Truthfully, he'd been more surprised that she'd ever said yes in the first place.

And while the party was always fun, he'd known that the odds of him and Lindsay actually making it there were slim to none.

He wasn't concerned when she didn't answer when he rang the doorbell. She was nothing if not stubborn and obviously didn't want to talk to him about her reasons for breaking their plans. And though he knew her refusal to come to the door was hardly an emergency, he didn't hesitate to use the key she'd given to him in case of one.

He took off his boots inside the door before making his way to the kitchen to put the bottle of champagne he'd brought in the refrigerator. The house was quiet, confirming that the kids were gone. Proof that she hadn't planned to stand him up, which made him feel a little bit better about the fact that she'd done so.

Was it his fault? Had he pressured her to say yes? He tried to respect the fact that she was grieving, but Nate had been gone for more than two years now, and Mitch couldn't help but worry sometimes that Lindsay was barely living.

"It's just me, Linds," he called out so that she wouldn't be startled by the creaking stairs as he made his way to the upper level.

She didn't say anything, but he thought he heard the exhale of a weary sigh from what he knew was her bedroom.

He paused in the doorway when he saw her sitting on the floor, her chin propped on her knees. Her long blond hair spilled over the shoulders of a fuzzy red sweater she wore with black leggings, and her face was streaked with tears.

His heart ached for her, but he kept his tone light when he said, "I was wrong."

She lifted beautiful moss-green eyes to look at him then. "About what?"

"I didn't think there was an emergency, but apparently a hurricane passed through here."

She managed a weak smile as her gaze surveyed the disaster zone that used to be her bedroom. "I can see why you might think that," she acknowledged.

"Not a hurricane?"

She shook her head.

"You stuffed your closet too full and it vomited all of its contents?" The drawers of her dressers were open, too, and mostly empty.

That got another subtle head shake.

"I was trying to find something to wear to the party," she finally confided.

"You want some help with the cleanup?" He didn't wait for a response before crouching to pick up the nearest garment, a blue velvet dress with long sleeves and a ruffled skirt.

She sighed again and pushed herself to her feet. "You shouldn't be here, Mitchell. You should be at Diggers'."

"We made plans to celebrate the New Year together," he reminded her.

"I don't feel much like celebrating."

"Then we'll not celebrate together."

"I'm in a seriously lousy mood," she warned.

He was pretty sure her mood was *sad* rather than *bad*, and, as her friend, he refused to let her wallow.

"Look at your feet," he suggested.

Her brows drew together. "What?"

"Look at your feet," he said again.

Though her expression remained skeptical, she tipped her head down and the corners of her mouth slowly lifted.

It wasn't quite a smile, but it definitely wasn't a frown.

"See? Red-nosed reindeer socks make everything better."

"Avenlea loves these socks," she confided, wiggling her toes.

"Who wouldn't?" he agreed, reaching for a discarded hanger for the dress.

"Don't." She tugged the garment out of his hand and tossed it toward the chair in the corner.

Her effort fell short, and the dress slid off the edge of the seat to pool again on the floor.

"Donation pile?" he guessed.

She nodded. "For the women's shelter."

He didn't mean to pry, but he wanted to understand what had led to the pillaging of her wardrobe. "It doesn't fit? You don't like it anymore?"

Now she shook her head. "The last time I wore it was to a Christmas party...with Nathan."

"Ahh."

He moved to pick up the discarded garment and drape it over the chair.

"And this one?" he asked, shaking out a sleeveless black dress that had been crumpled into a ball.

"I bought that one for the funeral." She swallowed. "I don't even know why I still have it. It's not like I was ever going to be able to wear it and not think, 'this is the dress I wore to my husband's funeral.'"

"I'm sorry," Mitch said gently. "I didn't realize my invitation was going to lead you into a minefield of memories."

"It's not your fault," she told him. "The closet was obviously overdue for a cleaning, and it's been a while since I've had a meltdown so that was probably overdue, too."

"You should have called me—I would have been here for you."

"I know," she said. "But I generally prefer to have my meltdowns in private."

"Are these meltdowns a regular occurrence?" he asked, sincerely concerned.

"No. In fact, I haven't had one like this since…June."

The day of her wedding anniversary, he'd bet.

"So…are you keeping any of this stuff?" he wondered.

"Yeah, but—" she waved a hand dismissively "—I'll deal with it later."

"Why don't we deal with it now? Then when you want to fall into bed tonight, you'll actually be able to find it."

With a sigh of resignation, she scooped up a sweater and began to fold it.

He held up a sparkly silver top for her consideration.

"Donate," she said.

Yoga pants went into the dresser; button-front shirts were hung in the closet; a lacy nightgown was snatched out of his hand.

"If you really wanted to be helpful, you'd go to the party," Lindsay said, tucking the intimate garment into a drawer.

"How would that help?" he wondered aloud.

"By allowing me to maintain the illusion that I didn't completely ruin your New Year's Eve."

"You haven't ruined anything," he assured her.

"I'm just not ready," she said quietly. "I know I should be...it's been more than two years...but I'm not."

"Grief doesn't operate on any particular schedule," he said, drawing her into his arms. "If you're not ready, you're not ready, and you don't have to apologize for that."

He stood six inches taller than her five-feet four-inch frame, and she dropped her forehead against his chest, her voice muffled against his shirt when she said, "Why are you being so understanding?"

"Nate was my friend, too," he reminded her. "And every once in a while, someone will say or do something that reminds me of him and I'll smile at the memory...and then I'll remember that he's gone and curse at the unfairness of it all. I can only imagine how much worse it must be for you, because he was your husband and the father of your children."

"I teared up in The Trading Post a couple weeks ago," she admitted. "In the cereal aisle, when I told Elliott to pick a cereal, and he grabbed a box of shredded wheat."

"I've never heard of a kid choosing shredded wheat," he admitted.

"He'd never had it before, but I think he recognized the box, because it was Nathan's favorite. In the winter—which was about eight months of the year in Moose Creek—he liked it with warm milk. And heaping teaspoons of sugar."

"So…did you buy the shredded wheat?"

"I did," she confirmed. "And then I went back the next day to get a box of Kix, because Elliott decided that shredded wheat was gross."

Mitch chuckled. "I wouldn't disagree with that."

She moved out of his arms then and reached down to pick up a T-shirt. "You're not going anywhere, are you?"

"Not before midnight," he told her.

"Not even if I kick you out?"

"You can try," he said. "But I'm bigger and stronger than you."

"You're also single," she pointed out, as she folded the shirt and tucked it into a drawer. "Which is why you should be out tonight, dancing and flirting with pretty girls."

"I'd rather be here with you," he said, and immediately winced at the backhanded compliment.

But Lindsay laughed. "I've never had to worry about keeping my feet on the ground around you."

"What I meant to say is that I'd rather be here with the prettiest girl in town."

She shook her head, but she was smiling. "What I am, right now, is hungry. Why don't you call Jo's and order a pizza?"

"Because everybody—and all of their cousins—orders pizza from Jo's on New Year's Eve, and I don't want to wait three hours to eat."

"Pizza in three hours beats no pizza at all," she said philosophically.

"I have a better idea," he said. "How about I go down to the kitchen and forage for food while you finish up in here?"

She nodded. "That works."

He started toward the door.

"Mitch?"

He turned back again. "Yeah?"

"Thank you…for knowing I needed your company even before I realized it myself."

"I'll always be here for you, Linds."

It was a promise he felt confident that he could keep.

Because he'd gotten over his teenage crush on her a lot of years earlier—he was almost certain of it.

Chapter Two

Lindsay followed the rich scents of tomato, garlic and oregano into the kitchen, her lips curving automatically when she saw Mitchell standing by the stove. She imagined any woman would smile to see a good-looking guy cooking dinner—and she had to admit, her best friend had grown up gorgeous.

The stereotypical tall, dark and handsome description fit him as well as the dark jeans, button-down shirt and vest he wore, but he was so much more than that. Along with the strong, hard body of a rancher, he had a gentle touch and a generous heart. She'd loved him for almost as long as she'd known him, and it was no wonder that her children loved him, too.

"I see you found the pasta sauce in the freezer."

He dropped a handful of spaghetti into the pot of

water already boiling on the stove. "Lucky I did," he said. "Because your fridge is woefully empty."

"I forgot to stop at the grocery store today," she confided. "Plus, I thought we'd be eating at the party."

"Well, I did put out some snacks, in case you wanted to nibble on something while we're waiting for the pasta to cook."

He'd opened a bottle of her favorite cabernet sauvignon, too, she noted, and poured two glasses.

It wasn't surprising that he was as comfortable in her home as his own. Especially considering that the house in which she was now living with her kids was the same house she and her sister had grown up in, and Mitchell, as one of her best friends, had spent plenty of time there with her, working on homework together or just hanging out. And since her return to Haven, they'd easily fallen back into their old routines, almost as if she'd never left.

She picked up one of the glasses and perused the appetizer plate as she sipped her wine. "You cut up string cheese?"

"Woefully empty," he said again.

She nodded an acknowledgment.

In addition to the circular chunks of cheese, he'd peeled one of the strings into thin strands and arranged them into a shape that looked something like a flower, added a pile of goldfish crackers to the plate, a glass ramekin of pimento-stuffed olives and a handful of slightly shriveled grapes.

Lindsay popped an olive into her mouth. "I bet you'd kick butt on *Chopped*!"

"What's that?"

"A TV show where chefs compete to incorporate four mystery ingredients into appetizers, main courses and desserts."

"Is that your idea of entertainment?"

"A mom cannot live on Nick Jr. alone," she told him.

"You never heard of ESPN?"

She pursed her lips, as if racking her brain. "It rings a bell."

Of course it did, because before she and Nate had moved to Moose Creek, Mitchell had been a fixture at their place, hanging out to watch the game, regardless of who or what was playing.

"The Sun Bowl was a good game this afternoon."

"I had a date with my closet this afternoon," she reminded him, as the timer buzzed.

"Based on what I saw—" Mitch turned off the burner and dumped the contents of the pasta pot into a strainer "—I think you should consider a new relationship."

"Or at least a new wardrobe," she said, spooning sauce on top of the plate of pasta he passed to her.

Mitch did the same with his own, then took a seat across from her at the table.

"To old friends and the New Year," he said, lifting his wine goblet.

She tapped her glass against his, then sipped her wine.

Mitch sampled his pasta. "Mmm…this is really good sauce."

"Nonna Delgado's family recipe," she said, as she sprinkled parmesan cheese over her plate.

"Judging by the stack of containers in your freezer, you plan on eating a lot of spaghetti this winter."

"It's one of Elliott and Avenlea's favorite foods," she said. "But those containers aren't all pasta sauce. There's also chili, beef stew and shepherd's pie."

"When did you find time to make all of that?" he wondered.

"It wasn't me—it was my mom. I swear she thinks we'd live on takeout if she didn't cook for us every time she visits."

"Or maybe she just likes to take care of you," he suggested as an alternative.

"And feels guilty that they moved away after I moved back home," she said, stabbing a chunk of pepper with her fork. "Either way, I don't argue with her about it, for fear that she might not feel inclined to stock my freezer."

He chuckled as he twirled his fork in his spaghetti. "I don't think they moved away because you came home—they were already getting the house ready for sale before…before you came back."

She didn't miss the pause and suspected that he'd been thinking "before Nathan died." But of course he didn't say it. Because most people tried not to remind her that she'd lost her husband, as if that might somehow allow her to forget. As if she didn't wake up every morning aware that she wasn't a married woman anymore but a widow and single parent to two young children.

"I know," she admitted now. "And maybe I should feel guilty that they put their plans on hold to stay through that first year for me and the kids, but I don't, because I'm not sure that I would have been able to manage without them or Kristyne or you."

"I don't know what I did," he said modestly.

"You were—and *are*—here for me. And for Elliott and Avenlea."

"That part's easy," he said. "They're great kids. And you're not so bad, either."

She smiled at that, then her expression turned serious again. "I'm sorry you're missing the party tonight."

"I'm not," he said.

"You didn't want to go?" she asked, surprised.

"Not as much as I wanted *you* to go," he clarified. "Because I'm pretty sure you haven't had a night out in more than two years."

"Not true," she said, as she pushed aside a slice of mushroom. "I was at Ridgeview Elementary School for the Season of Wonder holiday concert just a few weeks ago."

He chewed on a piece of sausage. "I meant a night out without your children."

"Yeah, it's been a while since I had one of those," she admitted. "But a night *in* without my children could be nice, too."

"Except that you're wondering what they're doing right now, aren't you?"

She glanced at her watch. "I don't have to wonder. Right now Elliott is watching the original *Cars* movie on Disney Plus with Grampa while Avenlea is snuggled with Gramma for story time."

"Or maybe they're both slurping Pepsi through Red

Vines and jumping on the sofa like it's a trampoline," he teased.

"You just got yourself taken off the approved babysitter list," she told him.

"If there's a list, I'm at the top of it," he said confidently.

He was right, because Elliott and Avenlea absolutely loved hanging out with "Uncle Mitch," especially at the Circle G Ranch where he lived and worked. And since the local minor hockey association had started its season in October, he'd taken Elliott to the ice rink at the community center for his hockey school session almost as often as she had. Which she really appreciated, because Avenlea hated being at the rink. Watching her brother push a puck around with his stick was *not* the little girl's idea of fun.

"Seriously, though, I feel lucky that Suzanne and Arthur make such an effort to enjoy their time with Elliott and Avenlea," she said. "Suzanne had a whole afternoon of activities planned for them—including crafts and games and special snacks."

"No wonder the kids love going over there."

"I always enjoyed visiting my grandparents' house when I was a kid," she said, smiling at the memory. "They had a closet under the staircase that was filled with toys and games for us to play with. And Grandma always made cookies that we got to eat fresh out of the oven. I still think of her whenever I have a warm chocolate chip cookie with a cold glass of milk."

"My grandmother says it's easier being a grandparent

than a parent, because you don't have to worry about enforcing rules and can just enjoy being together."

"That's probably true," she acknowledged.

"And now she's a great-grandmother times six—with two more great-grandbabies on the way," he said, referring to his cousin Haylee's twin pregnancy.

"I love my kids," she said sincerely. "But I'm so grateful they came one at a time."

They continued to chat comfortably about various and numerous topics while they finished their dinner and then tidied up the kitchen. Afterward, they took their glasses and the bottle of the wine to the living room, where Lindsay turned on the fireplace and Mitchell found a television broadcast of the New Year's Eve celebrations from Las Vegas. She plugged in the Christmas tree lights, too—"just one last time"—since the decorations would come off it the next day and the tree put out for pickup by the town, to be mulched for local naturalization projects.

"This is nice," she said, stretching her legs out toward the flames that ignited at the flick of a switch. Growing up, the fireplace had burned real wood and Lindsay still shuddered to think of the spiders she'd seen scrambling over the logs in the woodpile—or worse, felt crawling across her hands—when she and Kristyne were sent out to restock the bin.

"It is," he agreed.

"And quiet," she said.

He chuckled. "Do you want me to turn up the volume on the TV?"

"No. I'm happy to enjoy the quiet for a change." She

reached for her wineglass again, surprised to discover it was empty.

Mitch picked up the bottle and refilled it for her.

She settled back against the sofa again and sipped her wine.

"So...are you ever going to tell me what happened with Brittney?" she asked, referring to the girlfriend he'd split up with just before Thanksgiving.

He shrugged. "It's hardly a big secret—we just realized that we wanted different things out of the relationship."

"She wanted to get married and you didn't?" Lindsay guessed.

"She wanted to at least know we were moving in that direction and I wasn't sure that we were. Not after only six months together."

"Making a commitment after six months might seem hasty when you're twenty," she said. "But half a year should be enough time to figure things out when you're thirty-three."

"You're right," he agreed. "And I figured out she wasn't someone I wanted to spend the rest of my life with, but we parted on good terms."

"I guess that's fair. But you shouldn't be too picky," she cautioned. "There probably aren't many—if there are *any*—single women left in this town that you haven't already dated."

"Thankfully, the world is bigger than Haven," he said lightly.

Lindsay sipped her wine as she watched the fire.

"So…who is she?" she asked, after another few minutes had passed.

He frowned. "Who is who?"

"The woman who's getting in the way of you committing to anyone else."

"There's no other woman," Mitchell told her.

Ordinarily she would respect his boundaries and let the subject drop, but the wine had made her feel brave. Plus, she really wanted to know. Because he was a great guy, and she honestly didn't understand why he was still single.

"Is she married?" she pressed, unpersuaded by his denial. "Is that why you're not with her?"

He sighed. "You don't give up, do you?"

"No," she agreed readily. "Because I want you to be happy. You deserve to be happy."

"I am happy."

"Really?" She didn't even try to hide her skepticism. "Because you're hanging out with a widowed friend on New Year's Eve when you could be at a party."

"Yeah, but I got a free meal," he pointed out.

"Does it count as a free meal if you did the cooking?" she wondered aloud.

"Does it count as cooking if all you do is heat water to boil pasta?" he countered.

"In my book it does," she assured him. "Plus, you defrosted the sauce."

"Yeah, that was a challenge. Seriously," he said, when she laughed. "Your microwave has more bells and whistles than the control panel of a jumbo jet."

"When have you ever seen the control panel of a jumbo jet?" she challenged.

"I watch TV," he told her.

"Well, I think you did a great job with dinner," she said, letting her head drop back against his shoulder. "And it was a definite treat to sit down to a meal that someone else had cooked."

"I'm glad you enjoyed it."

"So…what about you?" he asked, after several more minutes had passed. "Have you thought about dating again?"

"Me? No." She shook her head emphatically.

"Why not?"

She twisted the rings on the third finger of her left hand—a constant reminder of the vows she'd exchanged and the husband she'd lost. "Because I'm a widow with two kids."

"Elliott and Avenlea aren't going to scare off any potential suitors."

"You're right," she agreed. "I'm the one who'd scare them off. I'm a mess."

"Yeah, but you're a hot mess."

She laughed at that. "Thanks… I think."

"And I happen to know at least one former classmate who's solely focused on the hot part."

"Really?" She sounded more surprised than curious.

He nodded. "I was at Jo's recently with some of the guys from high school and Austin Saddler expressed an interest in asking you out."

"Did he give you a note to pass on to me?"

"No, but he said I could give you his number."

"I'll pass," she said. "And isn't he married to Lianne Glover?"

"He *was* married to Lianne," he confirmed. "They've been divorced about three years now."

"I hadn't heard," she said.

"You weren't here," he pointed out. "Anyway, it was a fairly amicable split."

"If there is such a thing."

He shrugged. "They've got a seven-year-old son together and seem to be making things work for Hunter's benefit."

"Well, good for them," she said, still sounding skeptical. "But I'm not interested in dating anyone right now and, even if I was, I'd never go out with the guy who threw my favorite Beanie Baby into a tree at Prospect Park."

"I forgot that was Austin," he said, though of course he remembered the incident.

"Well, I didn't," she assured him. "And I didn't forget who climbed the tree to get Tracker the Bassett Hound back for me, either."

She reached out then to trace her fingertip along the inside of his forearm, where she knew there was a jagged three-inch scar—courtesy of the branch that broke when he was in the tree, hastening his descent and gouging his flesh.

"You cried when you saw the blood," he remembered, wanting—*needing*—to focus on something other than the completely inappropriate way his blood heated in response to her gentle touch.

Was it the wine? The occasion?

Why was he suddenly aware of Lindsay as a woman instead of simply the friend she'd always been?

She lifted her gaze to his then, her eyes twinkling with humor. "I cried because you got blood on my Beanie Baby."

"I did not," he denied. "I tossed it down to you from the tree, and *then* I fell."

"My hero," she said lightly.

"I'm nobody's hero," he assured her.

"You're mine," she insisted. "For a lot more reasons than rescuing Beanie Babies."

Before Mitchell could respond to that, Lindsay's cell phone buzzed against the table.

"The only person who ever calls me after nine o'clock is you," she noted, automatically picking it up to glance at the screen. "It's my in-laws."

She was already swiping to answer the call. "Hello?"

Mitchell started to rise, probably wanting to give her some privacy for the conversation, but she touched a hand to his arm again, a wordless request for him to stay.

"Hi, Mommy."

"Elliott." Lindsay exhaled a sigh of relief when she heard her son's voice. "What's going on? Why are you still awake?"

"I couldn't go to sleep without sayin' g'night." His earnest claim melted her still-beating-too-fast heart into a puddle at her feet.

"Does Gramma know you're calling?"

"No," he confessed in a whisper. "She's downstairs, watchin' TV with Grampa."

"So you snuck out of bed and into Gramma and Grampa's room to use the phone?" she guessed.

"I 'membered your number," he said, a hint of pride in his voice. "But I didn't hafta know it, cuz it's programmed into Gramma's phone."

"Well, I'm glad you called," she told him sincerely. "Because I don't think I would have been able to go to sleep without saying good-night, either."

"G'night," he said, getting straight to the point now. "I love you, Mommy."

"I love you, too, baby. Now go to bed and have sweet dreams and I'll see you in the morning."

"Are you comin' for breakfast?" he asked. "Gramma's gonna make pancakes."

"I don't know that I'll be there early enough for breakfast," she said, because she was looking forward to the rare opportunity to sleep in (or at least try!) and not be up with her kids at 6:00 a.m.—even if she was skeptical of it actually happening. "But I'll definitely be there before lunch."

For the past several months, Elliott and Avenlea had spent one night a month at their grandparents' house, because Suzanne had asked and because Lindsay's grief counselor had told her that it was important to nurture her children's independence as well as her own. Apparently, wanting to hold on tight wasn't uncommon after the loss of a loved one, but it wasn't healthy. So Lindsay had reluctantly agreed to a first sleepover at Gramma and Grampa T's—and the kids had loved it.

She hadn't loved it, but she'd survived it—even if she hadn't managed to sleep a wink because the house just felt too empty without Elliott and Avenlea. But they'd been so excited to tell her about their adventures when they came home that she couldn't deny it had been good for them.

For Arthur and Suzanne, too, who'd been devastated by the loss of their only child and were grateful to spend one-on-one time with their grandchildren, the only part of Nathan they had left. And when Lindsay had suggested that the kids might enjoy having one sleepover a month at Grampa and Gramma T's, Suzanne had been so happy and grateful, she'd actually cried.

So Lindsay had forced herself to stick with the schedule, no matter that she usually woke up in the middle of the night when the kids were away, her heart pounding with an irrational but undeniable fear inside her chest that they were gone. After which she'd end up in Elliott's bed, with one of Avenlea's teddy bears clutched against her chest. Even if she didn't manage to fall back to sleep, the worst of the fear would fade as she counted the hours until morning, when she could pick them up to bring them home again.

"Everything okay?" Mitchell asked, as his own phone pinged to signal a text message.

She nodded. "Elliott just wanted to say good-night."

He scanned the message and swiped to close the screen again. "And MG wanted to tell me that he was spending the night at Paige's so I shouldn't expect him at the ranch too early in the morning."

"Because of course your brother would want to rub it in that he's got a woman and you don't," she teased.

"Something like that," he acknowledged.

"So—are there wedding plans in the future for MG and Paige?"

He shook his head. "I don't think he's ready."

"Sounds like I've heard this before," she mused. "Maybe the unwillingness to commit is a Gilmore trait."

"More likely he never got over being dumped by Hope Bradford."

"The girl he dated in high school? The one who moved to LA to become an actress?"

He nodded.

"But that was—" she did a quick mental calculation, though not as quick as she would have done before her third glass of wine "—at least eighteen years ago."

"When Gilmores fall, they fall hard and forever."

"That's actually kind of romantic," she said. "Even if it makes me a little sad for Paige."

"I don't think you need to worry about Paige."

"What about you?"

"What about me?" he asked warily.

"Should I worry about you? Why haven't you dated anyone since you broke up with Brittney?" And then, as if the thought had just occurred to her, "Is it my fault?"

He frowned at that. "What do you mean? Why would you think it's your fault that I'm not dating?"

Lindsay shrugged. "Since I moved back to Haven, you've been spending a lot of time with me and Elliott and Avenlea. Anytime I need something, you're here—even when I don't realize I need someone, you're here. It must be hard to be there for anyone else when you're always holding the hand of your best friend's widow."

"You're more than my best friend's widow," he said.

"You're my friend, too. In fact, we were friends long before Nathan Thomas moved to town."

She nodded. "But that doesn't give me the right to monopolize so much of your time."

"If there was someone else I wanted to be with, I would be," he assured her.

"Well, I'm glad you're here. It's nice having someone— an adult—to talk to at the end of the day. Usually my night ends with the latest adventures of *Brady Brady*," she said, naming the title character of the series of beginning reader books that Mitchell had given to Elliott for his birthday.

He grinned. "He still likes those stories?"

"They're his favorite," she assured him. "So much so that I could probably recite *Brady Brady and the MVP* without opening the cover of the book."

"I think I've read that one, too," he said. "Though not as many times as *Goodnight Moon*."

"That's a classic," she noted.

They continued to chat until the bottle of wine was empty and the clock had inched close to midnight. Then they opened the bottle of champagne that Mitchell had brought, and when the fireworks shot into the sky over the Vegas strip, they wished one another a happy New Year and tapped their glasses before sipping the bubbly.

He leaned forward to give her a customary kiss on the cheek at the same moment Lindsay turned her head to peck his cheek.

Their lips collided.

The contact was fleeting, but the impact was startling. It wasn't just her mouth that tingled, it was every part of her, from the top of her head to the tips of her toes, and especially the parts in between.

For so long, she'd known nothing but emptiness and grief. Now, suddenly, there were other emotions coursing through her system. Surprise. Awareness. Desire.

The feelings were unexpected but not entirely unwelcome.

She looked at Mitchell, trying to gauge his reaction to the accidental kiss, wanting to know if he was experiencing any of the same emotions.

His expression was guarded, and perhaps a little wary.

But she saw something else in the depths of his dark brown eyes, too. Something that almost looked like a flicker of interest.

He held himself perfectly still, as if waiting to take his cues from her, to let her decide what happened next.

What happened next was that she took his champagne glass and set it down beside her own, then she leaned forward and kissed him again.

Chapter Three

If the first kiss had been a surprise to Mitch, this second one was a revelation. Not only because it was the result of deliberate action on Lindsay's part, but also because it was so unexpectedly and unbelievably hot. The way her mouth moved against his with both urgency and intensity, it was as if she wanted nothing as much as she wanted to kiss him. Which worked for him because, in that moment, he wanted nothing as much as he wanted to kiss her.

He'd always believed that kissing was one of the more pleasurable things a man could do with his mouth, and often a prelude to so much more. But not since he was a teenager had he found so much enjoyment in a simple kiss, and he knew he would have been perfectly content to stay right where he was, all night, just kissing her.

But Lindsay wanted more, and she telegraphed her desire by sliding her tongue between his lips and into his mouth. The already hot kiss became an inferno, making him burn with yearning. She hummed, a soft sound of satisfaction low in her throat that stoked the fire inside him.

And then somehow, without him having a clue how it happened, she was in his arms, straddling his lap. Her hands were linked behind his head, her soft breasts were pressed against his chest and her hips were rocking against his in a way that had all the blood rushing out of his head.

As if of their own volition, his hands moved to caress her thighs, the curve of her buttocks, and he said a silent prayer of thanksgiving to whatever celebrity had popularized leggings because the thin, stretchy fabric left nothing of her curves to his imagination.

And yes, he'd imagined her just like this, wanted her just like this. Even when he knew he shouldn't. At first, because they were friends and he worried crossing that line might interfere with their friendship. And later, because she'd chosen Nathan, and fantasizing about his best friend's girlfriend was a violation of the bro code.

Not only had she chosen Nate, she'd married him. Then they'd moved twenty-five hundred miles away and had two beautiful children together. And the only reason she was here now—and he was here now—was that Nathan was dead.

He would never be more than her second choice, if he was even that.

The realization should have doused his passion, but

it was difficult to care where he might rank on her list when she was all over him. Even if he'd been last, it only mattered that she was with him now. Rocking her pelvis against his, creating a mind-blowing friction that pushed him dangerously close to the edge of rapture.

He let his hands explore higher, stroking the sides of her torso, skimming the curve of her breasts. She sighed into his mouth and started to rock faster, threatening the tenuous grip he had on his self-control.

If she'd been anyone else, he'd be tugging her sweater over her head and dragging those stretchy pants down her legs in anticipation of satisfying what was apparently a mutual and almost out-of-control desire.

But she wasn't anyone else—she was *Lindsay.*

And no matter that she was the one who'd made the first move, he couldn't help but feel as if he was taking advantage of his friend. A friend who was still grieving the loss of her husband.

Dammit.

That was why he was desperately trying to maintain his slippery hold, so that the almost out-of-control desire didn't spiral completely out of control. That was why he grabbed hold of her gyrating hips and, gently but firmly, shifted her away from the danger zone.

She whimpered, a soft sound of protest that tempted him to throw caution to the wind and ease Lindsay onto the soft rug by the fire and finish what they'd started.

Then she opened her eyes, and it took only a fraction of a second for the haze of desire to clear and reality to come into focus again.

"Ohmygod." She lifted a hand to her mouth, her fingers pressing against lips swollen from their kiss. He could see the remorse and regret in her moss-green eyes, but he didn't want to hear her say that she was sorry for kissing him.

So he spoke first, before she could. "Happy New Year."

She seemed surprised by his willingness to downplay the intimacy of what they'd shared, but he thought she looked relieved, too. Grateful that he wasn't making a big deal out of the mind-numbing lip-lock.

Her hand dropped away from her mouth.

"Happy New Year," she echoed.

Which should have signaled a return to the status quo—except that she was still in his lap, those talented, tempting lips within easy reach if he just leaned forward—

He cleared his throat. "And since it's after midnight now, I should probably be on my way, because there are morning chores to be done on the ranch even on New Year's Day."

"Oh. Right. Of course," she said, sounding just a little bit flustered.

And then she seemed to realize she was still straddling him, because she quickly scrambled out of the way so that he could stand.

Lindsay could feel the heat in her cheeks as she followed Mitchell to the door, waiting for him to say something more—or something at all—about the kiss they'd shared. But he seemed engrossed in the act of pulling on his boots, then putting on his jacket—or maybe he was totally unaffected by what had happened between them in the family room (hard evidence to the contrary!) while she was completely churned up inside.

"Is that really all that's on your mind?" she finally asked. "Morning chores?"

"No." He took his time zipping up the front of his jacket before he looked at her. "Not all."

There was something there—a flicker in the depths of his gaze that might have been desire—that made her think he wasn't as totally unaffected as he wanted her to believe. But then it was gone, leaving her to wonder if maybe she'd only imagined it.

She swallowed. "Do you think we should talk about what just happened?"

"It was just a kiss, Lindsay," he said tersely. "I don't think there's anything to be gained from talking about it."

"Just a kiss," she echoed. So maybe she had imagined that flicker, but she hadn't imagined his response to her kiss, even if he had been the one to end it. "You're right. Why make a big deal out of something that was obviously nothing?"

"I didn't say it was nothing."

"Well, you're acting like it was nothing." And it was a blow to her pride—at the very least—that he was so easily walking away from something that had shaken her down to her toes.

"Would it make you feel better if I told you that I was hanging on to my self-control by a thread?"

"No… Maybe. If it was true."

He looked at her then, with so much heat in his gaze that it reignited the embers of the fire low in her belly.

"Or we could just pretend it didn't happen," she suggested as an alternative.

He nodded slowly. "That might be for the best."

"Okay," she agreed, not entirely sure if she was relieved or disappointed by his response.

Mitchell paused with his hand on the doorknob. "Are you going to be okay now?"

She felt her cheeks flush. "The champagne might have muddled my judgment for a few minutes," she said, aware that her prim tone was a stark contrast to the passion she'd exhibited on the sofa. "But I promise you, I'm not going to have another meltdown just because we shared a kiss that we just agreed to pretend never happened."

"I was actually referring to the fact that you'll be alone tonight because Elliott and Avenlea aren't home."

"Oh. Right." Her cheeks burned hotter. "Yes. I'm fine. I'll be fine. Okay, I'm a little bit flustered. And maybe a little bit tipsy from the champagne."

"You had a few sips. Plus the better part of a bottle of wine," he acknowledged.

"It's the bubbles," she said. "They go straight to my head every time."

He nodded, apparently willing to accept the excuse if it made her feel better. "Make sure you drink lots of water before you go to bed."

"I will," she promised. "Drive safely."

Lindsay stood at the door, watching through the sidelight as Mitchell made his way to his truck. When he'd driven away, she leaned her forehead against the cold glass, as if that might cool the heat still churning in her veins.

Oh. My. God.

She'd kissed Mitchell.

Not just kissed him, but climbed into his lap and wrapped herself around him, practically begging him to take her right then and there.

Of course Mitchell, being the gentleman that he was, had declined her alcohol-fueled invitation.

But maybe it was unfair to blame the champagne for her behavior—and his response. Maybe the bubbly had lessened her inhibitions, but it was the first touch of his lips that had compelled her to throw caution to the wind.

And maybe his rebuffing of her attempted seduction wasn't about his morals so much as an indication that he hadn't been tempted by her aggressive efforts at seduction. He'd been turned on—from where she'd been sitting, there'd been no doubt about that!—but not sufficiently aroused to want to take her to bed.

Or on the sofa.

Or anywhere else, apparently.

She huffed out a breath, fogging the glass.

She should be grateful to Mitchell for putting on the brakes. For understanding that she was dealing with a lot of emotions and not thinking clearly.

But she didn't feel grateful.

She felt rejected and foolish and more than a little bit guilty. Guilty that she'd been unfaithful to the husband who'd been gone for more than two years. Guilty that she'd taken advantage of a man who'd always been there for her.

But mostly, with this newly awakened desire still churning in her veins, she felt alive.

And confused.

Because the man who'd awakened that desire was one of her oldest and dearest friends.

Of course, her old friend was an incredibly good-looking man with a hard body and a quick smile that made women sigh and yearn. He was also a member of the wealthy and successful Gilmore ranching family and one of the most sought-after bachelors in town. Lindsay didn't think there was a woman in Haven who hadn't secretly crushed on Mitchell or his brother Michael—better known as MG—and quite likely one or more of their cousins, too.

But Liam and Caleb were both happily married now, leaving the single women who wanted to nab a Gilmore to scramble for the affections of Mitchell and MG. And while the brothers were happy to spread their affections around, neither had given any indication that he was ready to settle down.

Not that Lindsay was looking for a relationship. She was still trying to wrap her head around the surprising realization that she could be attracted to a man who wasn't her husband. Though she'd been certain a part of her had died when Nathan did, apparently it wasn't any of those all-important female parts.

She would always miss Nate, and she'd always be sad that he'd miss so many milestones in each of their children's lives. But she'd moved on—or was at least moving in that direction. She didn't cry herself to sleep anymore—except on Nathan's birthday and their anniversary and the anniversary of the plane crash that killed him. And okay, she'd cried after her shopping trip when Elliott had asked her to buy shredded wheat.

Not just because she missed him, though she did every day, but because she felt so alone. It wasn't only on birthdays or anniversaries that she was cognizant of his absence; it was that there was no one to share the trials and triumphs of everyday life. Whether it was something as simple as Avenlea asking to use the potty or as complicated as figuring out what wrench to use to fix a leaky pipe—and then calling the plumber.

She was getting used to being on her own, but that didn't mean she liked it. And though her kids kept her busy during the day, there were a lot of long, lonely hours between their bedtime and her own. It was during those hours that she missed Nathan the most, that she started to think maybe she wouldn't mind meeting someone new.

Then morning would come, and she'd get busy with the kids and disregard the notion again. Because she barely had two minutes to brush her teeth before she rushed out of the house, never mind time for a romance.

Maybe she could revisit the possibility when they were older, but right now she couldn't imagine it happening. New relationships simply required too much time and attention that she didn't have.

Unless it was a new romance with an old friend.

No. Absolutely not. She refused to consider it.

Sure, she and Mitchell would be able to skip all of the getting-to-know-you stuff that dominated the beginning of a relationship, but she suspected that Mitchell—

having recently broken up with Brittney—wasn't looking for a relationship any more than she was.

And even if she was looking for a romance, it would be a mistake to look at Mitchell, because he was one of her best friends. He was the one person who'd been there for her at every point in her life—not just from the day she'd married Nathan to the day she'd buried him, but countless days before and after and in between. And she wasn't going to risk that friendship for anything.

The frigid wind slapped at his face and burned in his lungs when Mitch stepped outside into the bitter cold early morning of January 1.

"Happy freakin' New Year to me," he muttered, as he tucked his chin into his collar and shoved his hands deeper into his pockets.

His breath puffed out in clouds and his boots crunched in the snow as he trudged toward the barn. Because, as he'd remarked to Lindsay the night before, animals needed to be fed and watered every day of the year, no matter the weather or temperature or even the disposition of the rancher.

Fortunately, between him and his brother and their cousins, there were plenty of capable hands to share the work. Unfortunately, he'd drawn the short straw and ended up with morning chores on New Year's Day.

Which shouldn't have been any worse than any other cold winter morning, because he hadn't been out particularly late nor overindulged the night before. But he'd tossed and turned for a long time before falling asleep, and it seemed as if he'd only just done that when his alarm started screeching at him to wake up again.

The single cup of coffee he'd gulped down before heading out of the former bunkhouse that he now shared with his brother—when MG bothered to sleep at home—hadn't provided enough of a caffeine kick to compensate for his lack of sleep, and the Tylenol he'd swallowed had done nothing to diminish the pounding in his head.

He wasn't hungover. He'd only had two glasses of wine with dinner and, several hours later, half a glass of champagne, because he knew he was driving. Lindsay had polished off the rest of the bottle of wine, so maybe he should cut her some slack with respect to what had happened the night before.

Of course, nothing had really happened.

Nothing except that they'd shared one incredibly hot kiss that had made him want so much more.

It wasn't her fault that she'd gotten him all stirred up—it was the wine that had fueled her actions.

And the press of her sexy body against his that had revived his long-dormant fantasies.

Sure, he'd thought about kissing her before last night. But that was years ago, when he was a teenage boy who suddenly discovered that one of his best friends was a teenage girl with curves in all the right places. But even then, he'd been reticent to act on what he was thinking. Maybe too reticent—but that was water long under the bridge.

He'd kissed a lot of girls in his thirty-three years— more than his fair share, some would say—but he'd never made a move on Lindsay. Well, not since he'd proposed to her when they were both ten years old, and that quick peck—and immediate recoil—hardly counted as a kiss. Obviously they'd both learned a lot since then, but never would he have imagined that a single kiss could generate so much heat and passion.

Thinking about it now, he realized that she probably hadn't kissed a man since her husband died—more than two years earlier. And he would bet the ranch that she hadn't been intimate with one. Maybe she took care of her own needs—and he definitely didn't want to let his mind wander too far down that tantalizing path—but from his perspective, a solo adventure was never as satisfying as one with a partner.

"Here you are," MG said, jolting Mitchell out of his prurient fantasy and back to the present as he sauntered into the barn—conveniently *after* Mitch had finished mucking out the stalls.

He wiped a hand over his sweaty brow. "Where else would I be?"

MG shrugged. "You were MIA last night."

"I wasn't MIA," he denied.

"Well, you didn't show up at Diggers' after you'd said you'd be there."

"Change of plans," he said, rolling back his shoulders and arching his back to stretch out the tight muscles.

"You hung out with Lindsay and the kids at her place, didn't you?" his brother guessed.

"Actually, the kids were with their grandparents."

"So just you and Lindsay," MG mused thoughtfully. "Now I get why you skipped the party."

"There's nothing to get," Mitch told him. "Lindsay didn't feel like going out, so we stayed in."

His brother nodded. "Because you wanted to make your move without half of the population of Haven watching."

"I did *not* make a move."

And it was true.

Lindsay had made the move, but he wasn't going to share any of that with MG, who would somehow twist the details to rib him mercilessly—because that's what brothers did.

Now MG shook his head. "Nathan's been gone for more than two years. What are you waiting for?"

"She's my friend," he reminded his brother—and himself.

"She's also incredibly hot. And if you try to tell me you don't see her that way, you're either lying or in denial because I know how hard you crushed on her in high school."

"Maybe I did," he acknowledged. "But that was high school, and I got over my crush a long time ago."

"Did you?" MG pressed.

"I stood up for her husband at their wedding," he reminded his brother.

"And got drunk that night."

"As if you've never overindulged at a party," he scoffed.

"You got drunk again the night before they moved to Alaska," MG pointed out.

"That was eight years ago—how could you possibly

remember something like that when I don't even remember what I was doing eight years ago?"

"You only wish you could forget," MG said. "I remember because I saw how it gutted you to say goodbye to her, knowing she was moving twenty-five hundred miles away and not knowing if she'd ever come back."

Uncomfortable with his brother's insightful assessment, he turned the tables. "You've been reading mom's romance novels again, haven't you?"

"As if you didn't read them, too," MG retorted.

Of course his brother knew that he had, because they'd passed the books back and forth when they were younger, giggling—and yes, aroused—by the explicit and intimate details.

"There was some good stuff in those books," he acknowledged. "I learned a lot from the love scenes."

"Is that where you learned to sidestep uncomfortable questions, too?"

"I don't recall a question—just you spouting some made-up nonsense about my supposed feelings way back when."

"Okay, let's skip to the present," MG said.

"Let's," Mitch agreed, with false enthusiasm.

"On New Year's Eve this year, when you had the opportunity to be at a party with an assortment of beautiful, single women, you chose to spend a quiet night at home with Lindsay instead. And somehow, I'm supposed to believe this is proof that you're no longer carrying a torch for her."

"Did they bring in a bus from out of town? Because

the last time I checked, there weren't that many beautiful, single women in Haven."

"You mean, that you haven't already dated," MG clarified, as Olivia muscled open the door and led Dolly, her palomino mare, into the barn.

"Or you haven't," Mitch countered, with a nod to acknowledge their sister's presence. "And if you want to talk about torches—yours has been burning bright for eighteen years."

"Are we talking about Hope?" Olivia asked, referring to MG's long-ago girlfriend who'd left Haven to pursue an acting career in Hollywood when she was seventeen years old.

"No, we're not talking about Hope," MG said firmly. "And Mitch is full of the stuff he shoveled into that wheelbarrow."

"So you don't have your DVR set to record every episode of *Rockwood Ridge*?" their sister challenged as she removed the horse's saddle and bridle.

"It's a good show," MG said, in defense of the popular weekly drama in which Hope played a recurring role.

"Uh-huh," Mitch agreed, as Olivia carried her equipment to the tack room. "But most people erase an episode after watching it. You save them until you can buy the season on DVD."

"Don't even try to deny it's true," Olivia said, rejoining their conversation. "Because Grams told me that she borrowed Season Two last week, because the finale is one of her favorite episodes. You know—the one where Lainey Howard, played by Hope Bradford, walks down the aisle to marry Thorne Chesterfield."

"I don't recall anyone inviting you to join this conversation," MG grumbled.

"I'm the little sister," she acknowledged. "If I had to wait for an invitation, I'd still be waiting."

"Why were you out so early this morning?" Mitch asked, steering the conversation in another direction to defuse the rising tension between his siblings.

"It was my New Year's resolution for both me and Dolly to get more exercise," she announced proudly.

"Wonder how long this one will last," MG said.

She huffed out a breath. "You could at least give me credit for making a resolution—I bet you didn't."

"Resolutions are for people who want to change," MG said. "I'm perfectly happy with my life just the way it is."

"Now who's in denial?" Mitch asked.

"I am happy with my life," his brother insisted.

"Paige isn't," Olivia noted. "We all saw her face at Christmas when she opened the box with The Gold Mine logo on the top and found earrings instead of a ring."

"They were diamond earrings," MG pointed out.

"Still not what she was hoping for."

"Well, she should have known better than to think that I'd ever propose with my whole family looking on," he said.

"She should know better than to think that you're ever going to propose—period," Mitch said.

"Because when Hope left town, she shattered his heart into a thousand pieces," Olivia noted.

"Ouch," Mitch said.

"But what's your excuse?" his sister asked, turning on him. "You've never let anyone get close enough to break your heart because you're still holding out hope that Lindsay will suddenly wake up one day and realize that she's in love with you."

"What do you know about love?" MG challenged.

"I know enough to tread cautiously," she said. "Because what I've learned from everyone around me is that when Gilmores fall in love, it's a life sentence."

It was the same sentiment that Mitch had expressed to Lindsay the night before—and why it was lucky that he wasn't in love with her.

Chapter Four

"I'm sorry," Lindsay said when her brother-in-law opened the door in response to her knock. "I know it's early, but I really need to talk to Kristyne."

Gabe Berkeley appeared to consider the request as he perused the tray of coffee cups she held in one hand and the paper bag in the other.

"I don't see a box with Sweet Caroline's logo on it," he said, sounding disappointed that, whatever might be in the bag, it obviously wasn't one of his favorite treats—apple fritters from the local shop.

"The bakery's closed today," she told him.

"Imagine that," he said dryly, stepping aside so that she could enter. "Almost as if New Year's Day was a holiday or something."

She chose to ignore the barb as she set the bag and

tray on the small table beside the door so that she could remove her boots. "But The Daily Grind was open, and they had s'mores muffins."

"Those are your sister's favorite, not mine."

Gabe disapproved of the concept of dessert for breakfast—apple fritters being the sole exception to his healthy eating rule.

"And she's the one carrying the baby," she pointed out.

"Which is why I already made her a spinach omelet for breakfast," her brother-in-law said.

"Then there's no reason you should object to her having a muffin for dessert," she pointed out reasonably.

"Is that decaf?" he asked, shifting his attention to the trio of cups in the tray.

"Only Kristyne's. You and I get the good stuff."

He flashed a quick grin. "Okay, you're forgiven for showing up before nine a.m."

She pried the cup marked with a B—indicating the coffee was black—out of the holder and offered it to him.

"And what did you have for breakfast?" he asked.

"I'm going to have a muffin."

Her brother-in-law shook his head. "I'll make you an omelet."

"Well, if it's not too much trouble," she said, smiling hopefully.

"Not at all. It's just beating some eggs."

"Thank you." She took one of the muffins out of the bag and balanced it on the lid of his coffee cup. "Cinnamon apple."

"I'll give you an A for effort," he decided.

She smiled and kissed his bristly cheek. "Happy New Year."

"Kristyne's in the solarium," he said. "I'll bring your omelet in when it's ready."

Lindsay made her way to the back of the house and the room with three walls and a ceiling composed of glass to welcome in the natural light. The decor her sister had chosen suited the setting: white wicker furniture with floral cushions, big ceramic pots filled with tropical plants and even a freestanding water wall. It was a room designed for rest and relaxation, and Lindsay knew that her sister spent a lot of time there, especially when her musician husband was busy writing or rehearsing in his soundproofed room above the garage.

"I thought I heard your voice," Kristyne said, when Lindsay stepped around an enormous banana plant and into view.

The expectant mom was wearing a tunic-style sweater and stretchy leggings with thick, fuzzy socks on her feet. Her honey-blond hair was piled on her head in a messy bun and her face, devoid of makeup, was glowing with happiness.

"You heard my voice and didn't even get up to say hi," Lindsay chastised teasingly, as she bent to kiss her sister's cheek.

Kristyne looked pointedly past her swollen belly to her legs, stretched out in front of her and propped up on the wicker coffee table. "The doctor has encouraged me to put up my feet as much as possible over the next couple of days to alleviate the swelling in my ankles, and Gabe is policing her directions."

"You assured me that everything was good at your last appointment."

"Everything *is* good," Kristyne insisted. "I'm fine, aside from some very mild edema."

"You should be drinking water," Lindsay noted, even as she reluctantly handed over the coffee her sister was gesturing for.

"I've been drinking water." Kristyne indicated the half-full sports bottle on the side table. "But I desperately want coffee—even if I know it's decaf."

Lindsay sat sideways on the sofa, so that she was facing her sister. "How are you feeling otherwise?"

"Fat."

Unable to resist, she reached over to gently rub the curve of her sister's belly. "You're not fat, you're pregnant."

"To-may-to, to-mah-to."

Kristyne opened the bag Lindsay offered, her gloomy expression brightening when she saw what was inside.

"But I really can't complain," she continued. "Gabe has been waiting on me hand and foot—and keeping the house tidy, too."

"Enjoy it while you can," Lindsay advised. "Once the baby is born, a tidy house will be a distant memory, you'll both be running ragged and you'll lament the days when you could actually close your eyes and relax for *just ten minutes*."

"I can't wait," Kristyne assured her. "I feel as if I've been pregnant forever."

"Be grateful you're not an elephant. They carry their babies for eighteen-to-twenty-two months."

"Maybe I am an elephant. I probably weigh as much as one these days. But I'm going to eat this muffin anyway," she said, tearing off a piece, "while you tell me about the party last night. And don't spare any details."

"Isn't one party pretty much the same as the next?" Lindsay hedged.

"Yeah, but since I didn't go out last night, I need to live vicariously through you." She popped the bite of muffin, rich with chocolate chunks and marshmallow bits, into her mouth and closed her eyes on a blissful sigh. "Mostly I want to know who went home with whom after the clock struck twelve."

"Then you're going to be disappointed, because I don't have those kinds of details," she confessed.

Her sister's eyes popped open again. "Don't tell me you skipped out before midnight." Then her gaze narrowed. "And don't you dare tell me you didn't go."

Lindsay sipped her coffee.

Kristyne sighed. "Oh, Linds. You didn't go, did you?"

"I *wanted* to go," she said. "But I didn't have anything to wear."

Which had seemed like a perfectly reasonable explanation the day before but now sounded like a hollow excuse—just like the other hollow excuses she'd manufactured to decline various invitations over the past two years. But she'd honestly intended to follow through when she'd said yes to Mitchell's invitation for New Year's Eve—right up until it was time to get ready for the event.

"That ranks right up there with 'I had to wash my hair' at the top of the list of Lamest Excuses of All Time."

"It's the truth," Lindsay said.

"You could have borrowed something from my closet," Kristyne told her. "God knows, none of my party clothes fit me anymore."

"Except that I didn't look in my closet until after I'd dropped Elliott and Avenlea off at their grandparents' house, and by then it was too late to consider other options."

"So you spent New Year's Eve alone?" Kristyne immediately shook her head, answering her own question before her sister could respond. "No. Mitchell wouldn't let you do that."

"No," she agreed. "Though I hate knowing he missed the party on my account."

"So what did you guys do?" Kristyne prompted.

"We ate spaghetti and watched the celebrations in Vegas on TV."

Her sister shook her head. "I don't think so."

"Excuse me?"

"I'm not saying you didn't have dinner and watch TV," she allowed. "I'm saying something else happened...something that brought you to my door the morning after."

"I think she came for a free meal," Gabe said, entering the room with a tray.

"Yours wasn't the only breakfast offer I had," his sister-in-law told him.

Kristyne waggled her eyebrows. "Do tell."

Lindsay rolled her eyes as she accepted the tray. "Suzanne was making pancakes this morning."

Her sister sighed, obviously disappointed. "That's *not* where I thought this was going."

"But this looks even better than pancakes," Lindsay said, eyeing the fluffy omelet filled with baby spinach and parmesan cheese and served with a side of sliced tomato. "Thanks, Gabe."

"You're welcome," he said. "And since I obviously interrupted a conversation about something that, truthfully, I don't want to know, I'll leave you two to chat."

Lindsay picked up the fork—on top of the neatly folded napkin beside the plate—and dug into the eggs.

"You really did luck out when you married him," she said. "Not only is he a hunky musician who loves you beyond belief, the man has serious kitchen skills."

"Nathan wasn't much of a cook, was he?" Kristyne asked, because she'd never been one of those people who tiptoed around saying his name, understanding that Lindsay's life with Nathan was something she needed to talk about, to remember.

"He was good at a lot of things, but cooking wasn't one of them." Probably because he'd made no effort to learn how to cook, preferring to let his wife be responsible for planning and preparing their meals. "Unless throwing steaks or burgers on the grill counts as cooking," Lindsay added. "He was happy enough to do that if I asked, but chop up vegetables to make a salad to go with the steak? Never."

"You should have expected that," Kristyne noted. "Considering he grew up with parents in traditional gender roles. Whereas Gabe was raised by a single father, so he knows a man is capable of doing it all—and he does."

"Even laundry?" Lindsay asked curiously.

"You should see the man wield an iron," her sister said.

"You're kidding."

Kristyne shook her head. "I'm not," she promised. "He even irons *my* clothes."

"That's impressive. Not quite as impressive as this," she said, lifting another forkful of eggs. "But still."

"Getting back to last night…" Kristyne prompted.

Lindsay took her time chewing, savoring the fluffy omelet—was that a hint of nutmeg she tasted?—and buying herself time to figure out what to say. Which she probably should have done on the drive over here, since the purpose of this visit was to talk to her sister. But it was a short drive, and Lindsay had a lot of tangled emotions to unravel.

She washed down the egg with a mouthful of sweet coffee before confessing: "Last night, when the clock struck twelve and fireworks exploded to fill the Vegas sky with light and color…I kissed Mitchell."

"So?" Kristyne was clearly unimpressed. "Everyone kisses everyone on New Year's—it's like a smooching free-for-all."

"No," Lindsay said. "I mean I *really* kissed him."

Her sister nibbled on another bite of muffin while she considered this revelation. "And then?"

And then Lindsay had climbed into his lap, pressed every part of her body against every part of his and almost come apart as a result of the delicious friction they'd generated together even with all their clothes on.

But there was no way she was going to share *those* details with her sister. Not because Kristyne wasn't a trustworthy confidante, but because Lindsay wasn't comfortable acknowledging the true extent of her shameless behavior. Kristyne wouldn't judge her but Lindsay was definitely judging herself.

"What do you mean—*and then*?" she asked. "Isn't that shocking enough?"

"The only shocking part is that it's taken this long for you two to hook up," her sister said.

"We didn't hook up," she denied. "And what do you mean—it's taken this long?"

"Please. The two of you have been dancing around your feelings forever."

"What feelings?" She was sincerely baffled by her sister's matter-of-fact statement. "Mitchell is one of my best friends. And he was Nathan's friend, too."

"Which is probably what held him back from making a move before last night," Kristyne acknowledged.

Lindsay swallowed another mouthful of coffee as she considered her sister's theory. But the fact was, he still hadn't made a move—she was the one who'd kissed him, forcing him to extricate himself from an awkward situation.

"So…how was the kiss?" Kristyne prompted. "Was it sweet? Sexy? Did it make your toes curl?"

Lindsay couldn't remember the last time she'd been kissed like Mitchell had kissed her. Of course, when you were married with a preschooler and an infant, you didn't waste a lot of time on foreplay. Moments of intimacy didn't have to be few and far between, but they were often quick and unexpected. As a result, she'd almost forgotten how much pleasure could be found in a kiss—until last night.

"It made my toes curl and my heart pound and all my other parts ache," she confided.

Her sister smiled. "That's the very best kind of kiss."

"Except that it never should have happened," she said.

"Why would you say that?" Kristyne asked, mystified.

"Because a kiss like that changes everything."

"Isn't that the point?"

Lindsay shook her head. "I don't want our relationship to change."

"Obviously you do, or you wouldn't have kissed him," her sister pointed out.

"I wasn't thinking straight," she said. "We had wine with dinner…and then champagne."

"The alcohol might have lessened your inhibitions," Kristyne acknowledged. "But it didn't make you do anything you didn't want to do." She wiggled her eyebrows. "And you want to do Mitchell Gilmore."

"I don't." She huffed out a breath. "I can't."

"You can and you should. Nathan's been gone for more than two years," her sister pointed out gently.

Lindsay nodded, her throat tight.

Twenty-seven months and seventeen days, in fact.

Or was it eighteen days now?

She sucked in a breath, stunned to realize that she might have lost track of the number.

Not that she'd been counting on purpose. It was more that she'd been focused on getting through one day at a time, and after that first day came a second day and then a third…

"It's okay to move on with your life," Kristyne said gently.

"I have moved on."

Her sister shook her head. "Moving isn't the same as moving on."

Lindsay considered that as she swallowed another mouthful of coffee, no longer tasting the sweetness.

"If you'd really moved on, you wouldn't still be wearing your wedding rings."

She automatically looked down at the emerald-cut diamond solitaire and matching embossed gold band on the third finger of her left hand—proof of her identity as Nathan's wife. "When we got married, I was sure it was forever… I never imagined that I'd take my rings off."

"And you don't have to take them off now," Kristyne said. "But you should think about why you're still wearing them. Is it habit? Is it because you still feel married? Or is it because they protect you from opening your heart again?"

It was an insightful question, and Lindsay realized that her answer might be all of the above.

Mitch spent the rest of the morning with his cousin Caleb, delivering grain to feed boxes to supplement the winter diet of the Circle G cattle. When they were done, Caleb rushed home to his wife and baby, and Mitch went to the empty bunkhouse and made himself a sandwich. After lunch, he considered taking a nap but opted for a walk instead.

He might not have thought he had a destination in mind when he headed out into the cold again, but he wasn't at all surprised to find himself standing in front of his childhood home only a few minutes later.

He knocked the snow off his boots outside the side door, wiped the soles on the thick coir mat, then hung his coat and hat on the hooks inside the mudroom.

"I don't often see you here in the middle of the day," Angela Gilmore remarked when Mitch made his way to the kitchen.

"Am I interrupting?" he asked.

"Of course not," his mom said. "I'm just making bread—we can chat while I knead."

He reached into the cupboard above the coffee maker for a mug. "Do you want coffee?"

She shook her head. "No, thanks. I've had my quota for the day."

Mitch filled his mug from the carafe on the warmer.

"So what's on your mind?" she asked.

"Do I really only come here when there's something on my mind?"

"Or nothing in your belly," she teased. "And since it's too late for lunch and too early for dinner, I figured you wanted to talk."

"I wouldn't say no to something from that jar on the counter," he said, referring to the ceramic Cookie Monster container that had sat in the same spot on the counter for as long as he could remember—and was always guaranteed to have some kind of homemade goodies inside.

"Help yourself," she told him.

He lifted Cookie Monster's head and reached inside, then pulled out a handful of chunky peanut butter cookies.

Angela sprinkled flour on her board, then scooped the dough from the bowl and turned it out, creating a puff of white dust. It would have been easier—and maybe even cheaper—to buy a loaf at The Trading Post, but for as long as Mitch could remember, his mom had made her own bread, and the yeasty scent of a freshly baked loaf always reminded him of her kitchen.

He nibbled on a cookie, savoring the soft and chewy treat, and washed it down with coffee, strong and black, while she began to knead.

"Do you ever use that mixer Dad bought for you?" he asked as he watched her fold and press the dough.

"Kneading by hand is better for bread," she said, then grinned. "And better for my arms, too."

"So it's not that you don't use it because a kitchen appliance is a lousy anniversary present?"

She chuckled softly. "No. While I would generally agree that jewelry is a safer choice, I know very well how much that fancy mixer cost because I'd been eyeing one for some time.

"And yes, I use it to cook for your dad, so he reaps the benefit of his gift to me. But I bought him tickets to a Dodgers game expecting that he'd take me with him," she pointed out. "Because after thirty-nine years of marriage, we know one another pretty well."

"And even after thirty-nine years, Dad tells the same story on your anniversary every year—about the day you first met."

She smiled at that. "He does like that story."

"Is it true? Did you really fall in love at first sight?"

"There was an immediate attraction," she acknowledged. "But love, real love, doesn't happen in an instant. It's like growing a flower from a seed. The blossom doesn't appear overnight—it needs tending and nurturing."

He considered that as he chewed on another cookie.

"Is there any particular reason you were thinking about the story now?" she asked.

"Olivia was giving me a hard time earlier because I've never had my heart broken."

"Which only proves that your sister doesn't know everything," Angela noted.

He lifted his mug to his lips and sipped his coffee.

"Because I was there at the church when Lindsay and Nathan exchanged their vows, and I saw your heart break," she continued, her tone gentle.

"It might have cracked a little," he conceded. "But that crack healed a long time ago."

"I hope that's true," she said. "Because you've been spending a lot of time with her since she came back. Not just with Lindsay but Elliott and Avenlea, too."

"They're great kids."

"Great kids who don't have a dad, and who might already be looking at you as a father figure," she cautioned, folding and turning the dough again.

He swallowed his last mouthful of coffee. "Are you suggesting that I should spend less time with them?"

"Of course not," she immediately replied, sprinkling a little more flour onto the dough. "But I'd be lying if I said I wasn't worried that you might end up with your heart broken again."

"Cracked," he reminded her. "And I got over my feelings for Lindsay a long time ago."

"Maybe," she said. "But I guarantee that whatever barriers you've put up around your heart won't hold up for long—especially not against those kids."

If it was a warning, it had come too late—Elliott and Avenlea had already taken hold of his heart, and there wasn't anything Mitch wouldn't do for either of them.

Truth be told, there wasn't anything he wouldn't do for Lindsay, either. Because he loved her, too, but in a strictly platonic sense this time.

One incredibly steamy New Year's Eve kiss notwithstanding.

Chapter Five

Arthur Thomas—a semi-retired district court judge—and his wife, Suzanne—a lawyer-turned-homemaker—lived on Miners' Pass, part of a newer development in the most affluent part of town. Their house was two stories of stone and brick with lots of windows and professionally landscaped grounds, and the judge's home office had a bay window that allowed him to see anyone coming or going. Obviously he saw Lindsay coming, because he opened the door before she could knock.

Though her father-in-law was almost seventy, he was a good-looking man with thick salt-and-pepper hair, deep blue eyes beneath bushy eyebrows and a trim physique that he maintained through regular use of the home gym and—in the summer months—frequent rounds of golf.

Lindsay used to tease Nathan that one of the reasons she'd married him was that she knew he'd still be handsome when he got older because he looked so much like his dad. Of course, Nathan never had a chance to get older, dying a few weeks shy of his thirty-first birthday.

"Happy New Year." She kissed Arthur's cheek as she stepped inside the door. "Are you so anxious to get rid of the grandkids that you've been waiting and watching for me?"

He chuckled. "Of course not. I just happened to see your car turn into the drive."

"You weren't in your office working on the holiday, were you?"

"I was," he confided. "I promised to deliver my judgment in a civil action on the first day back, and apparently it's not going to write itself."

"So much for retirement, huh?"

"I'm only partially retired," he reminded her. "Suzanne's idea, because she worried that I wouldn't know what to do with myself. At least that's what she said. Truthfully, I think she was more worried that I'd be in her way all the time."

"There might be some truth in that," Lindsay acknowledged, aware that her mother-in-law was very Type A and had specific schedules and routines that she didn't like to have interrupted—unless it was for the opportunity to spend more time with her grandchildren.

"Anyway, I'm sure you didn't come here to chat with me. Elliott and Avenlea are in the dining room, finishing up their breakfast. Or they *were* in the dining room," he amended, as Elliott—apparently having heard his mom's voice—came racing around the corner.

"Mommy! Mommy!" He practically flew down the hall toward her, his little sister close on his heels.

"Mommy! Mommy!" Avenlea echoed.

Lindsay's heart filled with joy as she knelt to catch them both in her arms and squeeze them tight. She planted noisy kisses on their cheeks as she breathed in the familiar scent of baby shampoo…and maple syrup.

Obviously they'd had their pancakes for breakfast.

"Were you good for Gramma and Grampa?" she asked.

"Uh-huh," Elliott said.

Avenlea nodded her head, her lopsided pigtails bobbing.

"So good Gramma made pancakes. With chocolate chips."

"Chocolate chip pancakes, huh? Your gramma must love you an awful lot."

There were more head bobs then as Suzanne came down the hall from the kitchen at the back of the house, where the doors opened up onto a gorgeous interlocking brick patio for outdoor dining, weather permitting. The sixty-seven-year-old looked at least ten years younger, with sable-colored hair stylishly cut in a long bob and makeup immaculately applied. She was fond of sweater sets and neatly pressed trousers and always looked as if she was ready to walk into a PTA meeting even if she was spending the day at home.

Lindsay was suddenly aware of the contrast of her own outfit—a baggy sweater with jeans frayed at the cuffs.

Suzanne greeted her daughter-in-law with a smile and an air kiss. "Coffee's fresh, if you've got time for a cup."

Lindsay thought about the mountain of laundry waiting at home along with a ridiculous number of holiday decorations that needed to be taken down and packed away for next Christmas. And then she thought about how lucky she was to have in-laws that she sincerely enjoyed spending time with. And because the dirty clothes and garlands and wreaths and nutcrackers would still be there when she got home, whether that was in ten minutes or an hour, she said, "Coffee sounds great."

"Did you want some pancakes?" Suzanne asked, leading the way to the kitchen. "It will only take me a minute to heat up the leftovers."

"Thanks, but I already had breakfast."

"Coffee—even with lots of cream and sugar—doesn't count as breakfast," her mother-in-law admonished, aware that Lindsay was frequently guilty of substituting coffee for the morning meal.

"I know," she admitted, as she dropped another teaspoonful of sugar into the cup that Suzanne had set in front of her. "But I stopped by to see my sister this morning, and Gabe made me an omelet."

"You did get an early start, then," Suzanne noted.

"I don't sleep well when the house is empty," she confided.

And she'd hardly slept a wink the night before, not because Elliott and Avenlea were gone but because she couldn't stop thinking about the fact that she'd kissed Mitchell. And when she'd finally managed to fall asleep, she'd dreamed of him—but in her dreams, they'd done a lot more than share a few kisses.

"How is Kristyne?"

Suzanne's question jolted Lindsay out of her reverie. "She's good. Impatient, but good."

Her mother-in-law smiled at that. "She isn't due until the end of February, right?"

Lindsay nodded. "The twenty-fifth."

"Expectant moms are always so anxious to hold their babies in their arms," Suzanne acknowledged. "And all too soon, our babies are grown and we never realize we're holding our child for the last time, until he won't let himself be held anymore."

Lindsay reached across the island and squeezed her mother-in-law's hand. "And then you have grandkids—and you get to do it all over again."

Suzanne blinked away the moisture that had filled her eyes and forced a smile. "You're right. Grandkids are a blessing and a second chance."

"Grandparents are a blessing, too," Lindsay assured her. "I hope you know how much Elliott and Avenlea enjoy spending time with you and Arthur."

"We're happy to have them anytime," Suzanne said. "In fact, we were thinking—*hoping*—that you might agree to let them stay with us two nights a month instead of just one."

Lindsay's instinct was to say no—because she hated how empty the house seemed when her kids were gone. But that was a purely selfish reaction, especially considering how much Elliott and Avenlea enjoyed their sleepovers with Gramma and Grampa T.

"It would be a treat for us—and a break for you," her mother-in-law continued, to press her case.

At the library, Lindsay sometimes overheard female patrons talking to their friends about how they were desperate for a break from being a mom 24/7. She couldn't really relate to their frustration, because being a mom was all she had left now. But although her kids were everything to her, she knew that they needed to be given opportunities to experience and explore the world outside 355 Winterberry Drive.

"I'll look at their schedules and see what we can work out," she promised.

"Thank you," Suzanne said gratefully. "Now tell me about the party."

"I didn't end up going," she admitted.

"Then you should have come here," her mother-in-law said. "No one should be alone on New Year's Eve."

"I wasn't alone," she said. "Mitchell stopped by."

"I'm glad," Suzanne said.

And Lindsay knew that she meant it, but she couldn't help wondering if her mother-in-law might feel differently if she knew about the kiss that Lindsay had planted on Mitchell at midnight.

"You've been friends a long time," her mother-in-law acknowledged. "Arthur used to refer to you and Nate and Mitch as the Three Musketeers."

Lindsay nodded, smiling a little at the memory.

It was true that when the Thomases had moved to town—or back to town, in the case of Suzanne, who'd grown up on Sterling Ranch in Haven but moved away to go to college—during the summer before seventh grade, Nathan and Mitchell had quickly become friends. Nathan wasn't too happy to share his new friend with a girl, though, and he'd balked at Mitchell's insistence on inviting Lindsay along whenever they made plans. But Mitchell had stood firm, because he and Lindsay went much further back, to the first day of second grade, after her family had moved to Haven.

Aware of her status as "the new kid," Lindsay had been outside at recess, quietly watching different groups of kids playing hopscotch and dodgeball and spinning in Hula-Hoops, wondering which group might eventually let her join in. But for now, they were all keeping their distance, and she was alone eating her Oreo cookies when the dodgeball got away, bounced near her feet, then smacked her in the nose.

Cody, whom she'd already pegged as a bully when she saw him shove his way in front of Sonja in the line for the drinking fountain, pointed and laughed, apparently finding it funny that the new girl was crying *and* bleeding. Tristan, who'd thrown the ball, ran over to retrieve it, mumbling a cursory apology before racing back to his friends. But one of those friends walked away from the circle to take her to the first-aid room.

"I'm Mitchell," he'd said, introducing himself while they waited for the school nurse.

"I'm Lindsay."

Which, of course, he knew because the teacher had introduced her to the class, asking the other students—most of whom had been in school together since kindergarten—to make her feel welcome.

He waited outside while she was examined, and by

the time she'd been cleaned up and given a baggie filled with ice to hold against her swollen nose, recess was over. But Mitchell invited her to play dodgeball with them when everyone went out again after lunch, and she had the distinct pleasure of being the one to knock Cody out of the circle.

After that, Lindsay and Mitchell were almost inseparable. When a teacher told the class to "find a partner" for cooperative assignments, they automatically looked for one another. When Mitchell didn't want to read the book he'd been assigned for a report, Lindsay had read it with him; and when she struggled with fractions, he helped her figure it out.

Then Nathan Thomas moved to town, and their relationship dynamic had changed.

"Can we watch *Paw Patrol*, Mommy?" Elliott asked, almost before they were in the door back at home.

The show about search and rescue dogs working together with a young boy to keep Adventure Bay safe was his absolute favorite—an affinity that was reflected in much of his wardrobe and most of his toy box. When she was a kid, she'd memorized the TV schedule so that she knew which of her favorite programs came on at which day and hour. Now it seemed as if everything was available for streaming all the time. But because there had been rare occasions when service was offline, she also had a collection of backup DVDs in reserve to avoid potential meltdowns. Of course, if the power went out, they were all doomed.

"Can we get inside first and unpack your sleepover stuff?" she suggested.

"Then can we watch *Paw Patrol*?"

"Actually, I was thinking maybe we could play a game after I get the laundry started," she suggested, because she tried to limit their screen time as much as possible. "How about Pop-Up Pirate?"

Elliott made a face. "We played lotsa games with Gramma and Grampa T."

So she let them watch TV, because she knew the program would keep them occupied while she took the ornaments and garland and lights off the Christmas tree. She got started on the laundry, too, making sure that the first load included Elliott's new *Paw Patrol* hoodie, because she knew he'd want it for his first day back at school—only three days away.

Of course, he'd need a lunch for school, too, which meant that she definitely needed to get to The Trading Post tomorrow to stock up on the kids' favorite treats and other essentials. It was a challenge to send a sandwich that he would eat because, like most kids, he was most fond of PB&J, but there was a child with a peanut allergy in the class so it was crucial that all parents sent only peanut-free lunches to school.

Another thing that Elliott liked were the prepackaged lunches with crackers and meat and cheese that he could then stack together, so she tried to keep a couple of those on hand for those days when she realized she'd forgotten to pack his lunch. At other times, she made her own, substituting grapes or apple wedges for the candy treat.

So she pulled her phone out of her pocket and started to make a list: bread, milk, eggs, OJ, meat, cheese, crackers, yogurt tubes, apple sauce. Of course, she'd add a lot more items to her cart as she pushed it around the store, but having a list helped to ensure she didn't forget any of the essentials.

Her phone pinged, signaling receipt of a text message while she was adding to her list, and her heart actually skipped a beat when she saw Mitchell's name pop up at the top. It was both a ridiculous and juvenile reaction, considering that she and Mitch had exchanged thousands—probably tens of thousands—of text messages over the years, and never before had she reacted in such a way.

But never before had he kissed her so thoroughly that she could barely remember her name the next day.

She tapped to open the message.

OK if I pick up pizza and bring it over for dinner?

He wanted to come *over*?

Her heart skipped another beat at the prospect of seeing him again so soon, but she wasn't sure if it was anticipation or apprehension. And how screwed up was that?

Because she *always* looked forward to seeing him. She was always happy to hang out with a friend who knew her better than almost anyone else and loved her anyway. And she knew that he did love her—just as she loved him, in the enduring but purely platonic way of two people who had been friends forever.

Now they were friends who'd shared a steamy kiss while locked in a passionate embrace, and she needed some more time to figure out what that meant for their relationship going forward. Because pretending it hadn't happened wasn't working so well for her.

But if she told Mitch that she didn't want him to come over, then he might think she was making a big deal out of what had happened the night before. And as he'd pointed out, it was just a kiss. And maybe a little bit of touchy-feely stuff along with the kissing, but certainly nothing that warranted getting her panties in a twist.

Except that just the memory of that kiss was almost enough to make her panties melt.

So she pushed the memory aside and refocused her attention on his message, determined to reply as if nothing of any significance had happened between them.

Depends. Are you planning to share?

He responded with an eye roll emoji followed by:

Of course.

She answered:

In that case...yes!

Be there around 6.

Sounds good.

And then, because she was in the laundry room, she wondered if she should change her clothes.

But why would she?

There wasn't anything wrong with what she was wearing. In fact, the jeans and turtleneck sweater were perfectly appropriate for an afternoon at home with her kids.

Maybe the sweater was a little big and not at all flattering to her figure, but she didn't need to try to make herself attractive just because a friend was coming over.

Besides, Mitch had seen her looking a lot worse. Such as when she'd had dental surgery to remove her impacted wisdom teeth. Despite telling him that she didn't want visitors—because she didn't want anyone to see her with her jaw swollen and bruised—he'd shown up at the door with flowers. He'd even stood stoically by with the bucket while she vomited the remnants of the anesthetic out of her system.

He was there, too, the first time she got drunk—cautioning her to slow down on the cosmopolitans she was gulping like Kool-Aid because they tasted so good and because she wanted to seem as sophisticated as Carrie Bradshaw and her friends. Of course, she hadn't listened to his warning, and a few hours later, he'd held her hair back while she'd puked into the bushes outside Diggers'.

Apparently throwing up was a common theme running through her worst moments.

And considering those moments, it was unlikely that Mitchell would be fazed by the coffee dribbled on her sweater, above the right breast. Except that the stain did draw attention to her breast, which she didn't want to do. Especially when just the memory of his hands skimming up her torso and brushing the sides of her breasts was enough to make her knees weak.

She dropped her head into her hands and muffled a frustrated scream.

This was ridiculous.

She was being ridiculous.

Mitchell had been her friend forever. Whatever had happened between them the night before—and it really was just a kiss—didn't have to change anything.

Not if they didn't want it to.

She tugged the stained sweater over her head and added it to the pile of dirty laundry on the floor, then grabbed another sweater from the basket of clean clothes. This one was a V-neck in smoky gray cashmere— a Christmas gift from Kristyne and Gabe.

"What's for supper? I'm hungry," Elliott said, when she came out of the laundry room with a basket of clothes to be put away.

"I hun-wee, too," Avenlea chimed in.

"Uncle Mitch is going to bring pizza for supper," she told them.

"Yay!" Her son punched his fist in the air.

"Yay!" His little sister echoed the sentiment and mimicked the action.

"Just cheese?" Elliott asked hopefully.

"I don't know," she said.

But she suspected that Mitchell would get a small pizza with just cheese, because he knew that's what the kids preferred. And he'd bring one with pepperoni, black olives and hot peppers, because that's what she liked— even if she'd forgotten her own preferences for a while.

She'd given up olives on her pizza when she was dating Nathan because he'd hated them with a passion and she'd really liked Nathan, and it seemed like a small sacrifice to make to be with him. After they'd been dating a while, she'd suggested that they could get olives just on half, but he'd shuddered at the possibility that one might accidentally be dropped on *his* "just pepperoni" half of the pie.

And although she'd occasionally grumbled that she missed having black olives on her pizza, she would have given them up forever if it meant she could have her husband—and Elliott and Avenlea could have their dad—back.

Chapter Six

Sharing a casual meal and easy conversation with Lindsay in the presence of her kids seemed to Mitch like the perfect opportunity to restore the status quo—if only he could stop thinking about the night before and how great it had been to finally kiss her. But she wanted to pretend it had never happened, so that's what he was determined to do.

Did that make him a hero or an idiot?

He didn't have a clue.

But he had pizza—so he grabbed the boxes off the passenger seat and headed toward the door.

"Uncamitch! Uncamitch!" The enthusiastic greeting came from Avenlea, who raced toward the door, blond pigtails bobbing and green eyes twinkling. She launched herself at him, confident he would catch her despite the pizza boxes he balanced on one hand.

Of course he did, easily scooping up the adorable little girl with his free arm. She rewarded him with a smacking kiss on the cheek.

"Pizza! Pizza!" was the chorus from Elliott.

"Can you tell they're happy to see you?" Lindsay asked, taking the boxes from him as he shifted the little girl onto his hip.

"Me or the pizza?" he wondered.

"Probably both," she acknowledged with a smile.

But it was a slightly dimmer version of her usual vibrant smile, making him suspect that forgetting about that midnight kiss was going to take some effort on both their parts.

Thankfully, the presence of Elliott and Avenlea didn't allow for awkward pauses or strained silences.

"Is it cheese? Did you bring us cheese pizza?" Elliott wanted to know.

"The small box is just cheese, for you and Avenlea," he confirmed.

The little girl tipped her head back against his shoulder and looked at him adoringly. "I wuv you, Uncamitch."

It was a common refrain from a child who freely expressed her love to everyone around her, but still it made his heart melt. Every. Single. Time. "I love you, too, Princess Avenlea."

She giggled at the nickname he'd bestowed upon her when she'd dressed up as Cinderella for Halloween the previous year. Lindsay had balked at her daughter's choice when the little girl grabbed hold of the blue dress in the costume store and refused to let go. Not that she objected to the idea of her daughter wanting to be the storybook character; she just would have preferred that Avenlea dress up as the scullery maid version rather than the transformed princess. Because, as she'd tried to explain to the toddler, it was important to understand that she'd have to work hard to get what she wanted in life and not expect a handsome prince to give her the keys to the kingdom.

But Avenlea wanted the fancy dress and sparkly crown. And when Mitch pointed out that Elliott had been allowed to pick a firefighter bulldog costume without getting a lecture on the perils of believing dogs could wield fire hoses, she'd finally relented.

"If Her Highness and her adoring subject would like to come to the table, dinner is served," Lindsay said.

Mitchell grinned and carried Avenlea to the kitchen, setting her in her booster seat and buckling the belt around her waist. The routine was familiar and easy, and almost convinced him that their efforts to restore the status quo could be successful.

"I wanted to make a salad to go with the pizza," she said, as she poured glasses of milk for Elliott and Avenlea. "But The Trading Post was closed today, so my fridge is still as empty as it was last night. Emptier, actually, because Elliott and Avenlea ate the last cheese strings while they were watching *Paw Patrol* this afternoon."

"The great thing about pizza is that it's a perfect

meal all by itself," he told her, as he lifted a slice from the larger box and set it on her plate.

"I don't know that the USDA Food Guide would concur," she said, peeling an olive off her slice and popping it into her mouth. "But it certainly tastes good."

"I wike Jo's p'za," Avenlea said.

"Like," she said, emphasizing the *L*.

"Wike," her daughter said again, nodding.

"I think you're focused on the wrong word in that sentence," Mitch remarked. "You should have noticed that she didn't say she likes pizza. She specified Jo's pizza. Not yet three years old, and she already has a discerning palate."

"Except that she's only ever had Jo's pizza," Lindsay said.

"Nuh-uh," Elliott said, speaking around a mouthful of dough and cheese. Catching his mother's eye, he quickly chewed and swallowed before continuing. "Gramma T made it once—from itch."

"Itch?" A smile tugged at the corner of Lindsay's mouth. "Do you mean scratch?"

"Yeah, that was it," her son agreed. "She promised it would be better than Jo's, cuz it was homemade." He shook his head then. "It wasn't."

"How did I not hear about this before now?" she wondered.

Elliott shrugged.

"Did Avenlea like it?"

Her son shook his head again. "She took one bite, spit it out and asked for Jo's."

"Definitely a discerning palate," Mitch said, as the

little girl took another big bite of her pizza. "And now you know why Suzanne didn't tell you the story."

"That could be," Lindsay agreed, reaching into the box for a second slice. "And thank you for this—I didn't realize how hungry I was until I started eating."

"Because you don't slow down long enough to eat half the time," he noted.

"I did miss lunch today," she confided.

"But I'll bet Elliott and Avenlea didn't."

"How could I ever forget to feed them when they're constantly telling me they're hungry?"

"So why didn't you eat when they did?"

"Because I was taking down Christmas decorations. And I wasn't in the mood for a peanut butter and jelly sandwich."

He shook his head. "I hope you're planning on grocery shopping tomorrow."

"We'll be waiting outside The Trading Post for it to open."

"And what will you have for breakfast before you go?"

"Leftover pizza?" she suggested hopefully.

He laughed even as his hand instinctively lifted toward her face. "You've got sauce—" he brushed his thumb over the spot beside her mouth "—here."

It was the automatic gesture of a friend who felt comfortable letting her know when she had spinach in her teeth or an unknown substance on the butt of her pants after a trip to the park.

But this time, Lindsay's breath caught as her eyes locked with his. And Mitch's pulse thrummed beneath his skin, vibrating awareness through every inch of his body. And suddenly, neither of them was able to pretend the kiss had never happened.

His gaze dipped to her mouth, remembering the silky texture of her lips, the seductive flavor of her kiss, the sweet torture of her soft curves—

"Avenlea's got sauce on her face, too," Elliott said, breaking the sensual spell that had wrapped around them.

Mitch drew back, exhaling a shaky breath, and looked at the little girl who, sure enough, had red smeared around her mouth almost from ear to ear.

"I think someone's definitely going to need a bath after dinner," Lindsay said.

"Me! Me!" Avenlea said.

"Yes, you," her mom agreed.

"Not me," Elliott said.

"Just because you don't have pizza sauce all over your face doesn't mean you can skip your bath."

"But I had a bath last night at Gramma and Grampa T's."

"Well, then, I guess you won't need another one until Valentine's Day."

"Really?" he said, sounding hopeful.

"Not really."

He sighed wearily.

"Come on," she said. "Let's get the kitchen tidied up and get you two ready for bed."

"Can't we stay up a little bit longer?" Elliott pleaded.

She shook her head. "We've been a little too lax

about your bedtime over the holidays, and we need to get you back on schedule to get ready for school."

"I don't even know what *lax* means," Elliott protested.

"It means relaxed."

"But you always say it's good to relax."

"About some things," she agreed. "But routines are important, too."

"Why can't a later bedtime be part of the routine?"

Honestly, the kid had some impressive negotiating skills for a five-year-old.

"You already have a later bedtime than your sister," Lindsay pointed out.

"Because she's still a baby."

"Am not," Avenlea protested, though her words might have been more convincing if she hadn't had to take her thumb out of her mouth to reply.

"Are too," Elliott insisted.

"When do you go back to school?" Mitch asked, in an effort to avoid the familiar "am not/are too" sibling argument that he knew from experience with his own brother and sister could go on in perpetuity.

"Monday," Elliott said, obviously excited about returning to school and seeing his friends.

Of course, all kids loved school when they were in kindergarten, and according to his cousin's wife—who was Elliott's teacher this year—the new play-based curriculum meant that most kids were having so much fun they didn't even realize they were learning.

"I wanna go to 'chool," Avenlea said.

"I know," Lindsay acknowledged. "And when you're four, you will."

"And when you're fourteen, you'll be saying, 'Do I hafta go to school?'" Mitch told her.

Avenlea's little brow furrowed as she considered his warning.

"In the meantime, you get to go to swimming school," her mom reminded her.

"I wike swimmin'."

"And you're getting to be a really good swimmer," Lindsay said encouragingly.

"Uncamitch swim wif us."

"Uncle Mitch will be working when we're at the pool."

Avenlea shook her head. "Swim at Uncamitch's."

"Could she be talking about the pond at the Circle G?" Mitch wondered, though doubtful that the little girl would recall an event that had taken place five months earlier.

"Do you remember going swimming at the ranch last summer?" Lindsay asked.

Now Avenlea nodded. "Wif Uncamitch."

"Yes, we did," her mom agreed.

"But the water in the pond is frozen right now, because it's winter," Mitch explained. "You might be able to skate on it, but you can't swim in it."

"'Kate at Uncamitch's?"

"You want to learn how to skate?"

She nodded again. "Wike Ew-ee-it."

"Well, it's going to take a few lessons before you can skate like Elliott," he said. "But we can get you out on the pond, if you want."

"Want," she confirmed.

"Do you know what I want?" Lindsay asked her, as she unbuckled her daughter's safety strap.

"Go 'katin'?" Avenlea guessed.

"No." Her mom lifted the little girl into her arms. "I want *you* to have your bath and get ready for bed."

"But I not s'eepy." The little girl's protest was followed by a big yawn as she dropped her head onto Lindsay's shoulder.

The pizza had been a good idea, Mitch decided, as mom and daughter headed upstairs for bath time. After twenty-five years of friendship, he knew Lindsay well enough to know that if he gave her too much time and space to think about the kiss they'd shared, it would end up becoming a big thing between them. Plus, as he'd remarked to his mother earlier, she had great kids, and he really enjoyed spending time with them.

When he sat down at the table for the meal, it was almost too easy to imagine that they could be a family. But as he relaxed on the sofa, near where Elliott was driving his Matchbox cars around on his play mat designed to replicate a city center, complete with roads and greenspaces and buildings, there was no ignoring the fact that Lindsay's kids were also Nathan's kids.

Elliott was the spitting image of his dad, with Nathan's curly dark hair, narrow face, thick brows and straight nose. It was only his eyes that he'd inherited from his mom—both the shape and the mossy-green color. Avenlea, on the other hand, was every inch her mom's daughter, with the same pale blond hair and green eyes, and a sweet smile that never failed to tug at his heart.

While Elliott played with his cars, he regaled Mitch with stories about his Christmas holidays, about how Gramma and Grampa D came to stay for two whole weeks, and Gramma made cookies that she let them decorate with colored icing and sugar, and Grampa took them sledding. And about their visit to the fire station to see Santa Claus—and how Avenlea was too scared to sit on Santa's lap until Mommy went with her. (Mitch would love to see a picture of that!) They even made a trip to the antiques and craft market so that they could pick out presents to wrap and put under the tree for Mommy. Avenlea picked out a pair of fuzzy socks with reindeer faces on top of the feet—obviously the same socks that she'd been wearing the day before—and Elliott got her a book with blank pages that she could write in.

Mitch knew that Marilyn and Jackson Delgado had been in Haven until the thirtieth, and then flown back to Phoenix for the New Year's party at the community center in their retirement village. He'd enjoyed a brief visit with them the day before Christmas Eve, when he stopped by to drop off his presents for the kids. Though they seemed confident that they'd made the right decision when they'd moved south, Marilyn confided that they missed the grandchildren like crazy. Thankfully, they were able to keep in touch via Skype, so they could see Elliott and Avenlea rather than just talk to them. They'd also told him that they were planning to come back again in February—or March—depending on when Kristyne had her baby, and then again in the summer for a few weeks, as they'd done the previous year.

"Did you get new cars for Christmas?" Mitch asked, as Elliott took inventory of his fleet.

"Gramma gave 'em to me yesterday. They used to be my dad's."

"It looks like a pretty cool collection," he noted.

"This is a Camaro," Elliott said, pointing first to a yellow sports car and then a candy-apple red vehicle. "And this is a classic Mustang."

"What's this one?" He picked up a green van with a mostly faded but familiar logo on the side panel.

The boy shrugged.

"I think it's the Mystery Machine," Mitch told him.

"What's that?" Elliott asked.

"You don't watch *Scooby Doo*?"

"Who?"

He sighed and returned the vehicle to its place in the specific arrangement on the floor. "Kids these days have no idea what they're missing."

"Don't you mean meddling kids?"

Mitch grinned as he glanced up to see Lindsay had returned. "See? Your mom knows her classic cartoons."

"*Classic* is just a fancy word for old," Elliott said.

"Who told you that?" Lindsay asked him.

"Gramma T."

"Well, it's not really that simple," she said.

"But in this case, it's true," Mitch acknowledged.

"Anyway, it's time for you to put all your *classic* cars away and have your bath," Lindsay said to her son.

"And it's probably time for me to head out," Mitch said, not wanting to overstay his welcome.

"Actually, if you're not in a rush…" Lindsay began.

"What do you need?"

"Avenlea has requested that you read her bedtime story tonight."

"Me?" he asked, surprised.

She shrugged. "She likes the way you do the voices for the characters in *The Gruffalo*."

"And that stings your pride, just a little bit, doesn't it?" he teased.

"That she wants you to read about a monster with a poisonous wart on his nose?"

"Okay, that stings more than a little."

She laughed and nudged him with her shoulder as they walked side by side up the stairs together.

And if he felt as if he was walking in his friend's shadow, well, that was his issue to deal with on his own time.

Three days later, Lindsay was standing outside the fence that bordered the kindergarten play area, waving to Elliott as he raced to line up in response to the bell. Her son, happy to be back at school with his friends, never looked back.

"It's hard, isn't it?"

She turned to the man she hadn't realized was standing beside her, his hands tucked into the pockets of a blue ski jacket. He had short, light brown hair, with just a hint of gray at the temples and brown eyes with crinkles at the corners. He looked vaguely familiar—

no doubt she'd seen him at drop-off or pickup before, though she was certain they'd never been introduced.

"I'm sorry?"

"I was just remarking how difficult it is, to watch your child race off into the world," he clarified. "On the one hand, you're proud that they have the confidence to tackle the unknown. On the other, you can't help but feel a little superfluous, because you've done your job as a parent so well that they don't need you every minute of every day anymore."

"Nailed it," she admitted.

"A word of warning," he told her. "It's even harder when it's your youngest—or only—child." He inclined his head toward Avenlea, the little girl's mittened hand clutched tightly within her own. "At least you've still got one who sees you as the center of her world."

"How many kids do you have?"

"Three. Mason's the youngest."

"So he has older brothers or sisters who can look out for him as he navigates the perils of kindergarten?"

"He's got one of each, but they're not here. They're in high school."

"Oh."

He nodded. "My wife and I started young, and Mason was an effort to restore the dying spark in our marriage." He shrugged. "We're divorced now, but we got another great kid out of the deal. Or maybe I should say that *I* got another great kid, because she lives in Colorado now where she manages some posh ski resort, and I'm here with the kids."

"I'm sorry—not that you got custody," she hastened to clarify. "About the divorce, I mean."

He shrugged. "It wasn't how I envisioned things working out when we got married. Then again, I don't imagine you ever thought you'd end up a young widow, either."

"Obviously someone's been telling tales outside of school," she remarked lightly.

"I saw you at the holiday assembly and asked Debby Jensen who you were," he confided now. "She told me about the passing of your husband. That's why I told you about my divorce. I don't usually dump that information on a stranger at a first meeting, but I wanted to put us on equal footing."

"Thank you?"

He smiled. "By the way, I'm Parker Ross. Dad of Mason, who's in Mrs. Gilmore's class with your son, Elliott."

"Lindsay Thomas." She shook the proffered hand. "But of course, you know that already."

"I do," he confirmed.

"And this is Avenlea," she said, introducing her daughter.

"It's nice to meet both of you." He glanced down at the little girl. "Do you have time for a cup of coffee, Avenlea? Or do you have places to go?"

The little girl made a face; he laughed.

"Hot chocolate?" he suggested as an alternative.

Avenlea nodded.

"Unfortunately, we do have places to go," Lindsay said. "Avenlea's got a swimming lesson this morning and we need to get over to the community center or we're going to be late."

"Maybe another time?" he asked.

"Maybe," she agreed, meaning "probably not ever."

But then she considered that her explosive reaction to a simple kiss on New Year's Eve might have been a sign that she was ready to move on. And since she and Mitchell had agreed to pretend the kiss had never happened, if she ever wanted to be in a relationship again, she was going to have to put herself out there.

So what if there were no immediate sparks with Parker? Since when were sparks required to enjoy a hot beverage with someone?

"Actually, let's change that 'maybe' to a 'definitely,'" she decided.

"Yeah?" He flashed a quick grin. "You say when and where."

"Wednesday morning, ten-thirty at The Daily Grind?"

"I'll be there," he promised.

"You don't have to check a work schedule or something?" she asked curiously.

"Want to be sure I'm gainfully employed before coffee leads to dinner?" he teased.

"I'm sorry," she immediately apologized. "That was rude, wasn't it?"

"Not rude," he said. "Just not very subtle."

"I'm sorry," she said again. "I'm not very good at this."

"Making conversation?" he teased.

"Meeting new people," she clarified.

"It's not one of my strengths, either," he confided. "And in the interest of alleviating any concerns, I'll confirm that I do have a job. I work in IT support from home, so my hours are completely flexible."

"That's lucky," she said.

"Very," Parker agreed. "Because it means I can take a coffee break at ten-thirty Wednesday morning."

"I'll see you then," Lindsay promised.

Chapter Seven

Lindsay had always believed that the library was a magical place. As soon as she was able to read and discovered the power of words to transport her to different worlds, it had become her favorite place to visit. It was always quiet, it smelled like books and it was filled with stories. So many wonderful stories.

Library Day—always capitalized in her mind—had been her favorite day at school, because she'd return a book that had been read and reread countless times and take home a brand-new one to read and reread. She enjoyed all kinds of stories—nonfiction and fiction—because it was as interesting to read about real people as imaginary ones.

The Magic Tree House books had been some of her favorites when she was younger, and they were still a popular item in the library catalog today, albeit less so than *Junie B. Jones* and *Ready, Freddy!* But as she perused the stacks in the children's section, searching through familiar authors such as Sandra Boynton, Beverly Cleary, Roald Dahl, Robert Munsch, Shel Silverstein and Dr. Seuss, she found herself reflecting on the chain of events that had led to her opportunity to work at the local library.

She'd been lucky, when she came back to Haven, that Hazel Hemingway—who'd been the librarian for a lot longer than Lindsay had been alive—was ready to cut back her hours. Maybe *lucky* wasn't the right word, considering the reason for Lindsay's return, but it had at least been fortuitous timing.

Of course, being a working mom meant having to put her daughter in day care—and her son, too, when he wasn't at school. Her mother-in-law had tried to convince Lindsay to let Avenlea stay with her, but Lindsay believed it was important for the little girl to be with kids her own age, to learn to play and share.

"Is everything okay?" Quinn asked. "You seem a little distracted this morning."

"Sorry," Lindsay apologized automatically as she pulled *The One in the Middle is the Green Kangaroo* off the shelf and added it to the growing pile on the table where Avenlea sat with a box of fat crayons and some coloring pages, pretending she was at school "wike Ew-ee-it."

Since Lindsay had started working at the library, she'd become good friends with Quinn Ellison—the driver of the local bookmobile who lived in Cooper's Corners. The twenty-nine-year-old loved meeting people of all ages and backgrounds—even those who wondered why she didn't seem to have any greater ambition in life than to drive around with a bus full of books. Of course, those people didn't realize that Quinn's part-time driving job was really just a hobby for the best-selling novelist.

"Don't be sorry—tell me what's going on," her friend urged.

"It's nothing," she said.

"Let me be the judge of that," Quinn advised with a wink. "You never know what might be fodder for my next book."

"I guarantee that nothing about my life would interest your readers."

"Even the writer is growing bored now, so spill."

"Okay," Lindsay agreed. "When I dropped Elliott off at school this morning, one of the other parents—a dad—asked me to go for coffee."

"Did you say yes?"

She nodded.

"So you've got a date," her friend said, grinning. "Good for you."

"Is coffee a date?" Lindsay wondered.

"It's a date," Quinn insisted. And then, "Is he cute?"

"I'm not sure that *cute* is a word that should be applied to anyone over the age of thirty," she cautioned.

"Which doesn't answer my question."

"He's kind of handsome, I guess."

Her friend rolled her eyes. "You guess?"

"He *is* handsome," she said. Maybe he wasn't quite as tall as Mitchell, and his shoulders weren't nearly as broad as the rancher's nor his jaw as strongly defined and…why was she comparing Parker to Mitchell? Even if her friend was one of the hottest bachelors in town, and probably the absolute best kisser and—

Aargh! She really needed to stop thinking about Mitchell!

"And he has a nice smile," she said, refocusing her thoughts on Parker.

"So when is this date?" Quinn asked. "And where?"

"Wednesday. The Daily Grind. But now I'm wishing that I'd agreed to have coffee this morning so I wouldn't have to spend the next two days thinking about it."

"Why didn't you agree to coffee this morning?"

"Because Avenlea had a swimming lesson."

"Which I'm sure she would have happily sacrificed in the interest of romance."

"Have you met my daughter?" Lindsay asked dryly.

Quinn chuckled. "I have, and I know that she can be bribed with chocolate."

Avenlea's head shot up. "Choc'ate?" she asked hopefully.

"See?" Quinn said to Lindsay, as she pulled a treat-size Kit Kat out of her pocket.

The little girl held out the hand not holding the red crayon. "P'ease?"

Quinn gave her the chocolate. "But you have to save it until later, when Mommy says, okay?"

"'Kay," Avenlea promised.

Lindsay shook her head as she continued to help her friend collect the books on a list carefully curated to reflect the preferences of her regular patrons, who ranged in age from two to ninety-two.

"Well, at least you said yes to Wednesday," Quinn said. "Because you have to take the first step sometime."

"Says who?" Lindsay challenged.

"Says me." Her friend's tone was firm. "You're too young to spend the rest of your life alone."

"It's hard to be alone with a five-year-old and almost-three-year-old in the house," Lindsay pointed out. "I can't even shower without one of them interrupting."

"You know what I mean," Quinn chided. "Plus, your kids are eventually going to grow up and move out, and then you really will be alone."

"I think I've still got a few years before that happens," she said dryly.

"A few," her friend agreed. "So…what time do you want a fake emergency text on Wednesday? Around ten forty-five?"

Lindsay frowned. "Why would you send me a fake emergency text?"

Quinn shook her head. "You really have been out of the dating game a long time, haven't you?"

"Only because Nathan and I both agreed not to date other people while we were married," she remarked dryly

"The fake emergency text is sent so that the friend on the date has an excuse to escape if the guy is a disaster."

"It's *coffee*," Lindsay said again. "The only disaster I can imagine is if The Daily Grind is out of whipped cream for my café mocha."

"Whipped cream on a first date?" Quinn shook her head. "I didn't realize you were such a brazen hussy."

"But now I'm wondering what kind of fake emergency you might come up with," she said, ignoring her friend's comment. "Just in case you do text me around ten forty-five on Wednesday about a real emergency."

"Work-related emergencies are usually best, to avoid the potential of creating any real panic." Quinn's ready response convinced Lindsay that she'd done this before.

"What kind of work-related emergency happens at the library?" she wondered.

Quinn turned to look at the shelf of books behind her. "Right here," she said, her finger sliding across the adjacent spines of two books. "*Ramona the Pest* should come after *Ramona the Brave*. These books are clearly out of order, and without order, there is only chaos."

"They're not in strict alphabetical order," Lindsay allowed. "But the Ramona series is in chronological order."

"Chaos," Quinn said again, making Lindsay laugh.

She had a date.

Only four days after she'd kissed him, Lindsay apparently had agreed to a date with someone else. Another single parent from the school, or so Mitch had been told.

He mulled over the information, not sure how he was supposed to feel about it. Not sure what to think about the fact that he'd suffered through four days of cold showers because of the kiss-that-never-happened while she'd suddenly decided that she was ready to start dating.

But maybe he should hear Lindsay's side of the story before jumping to conclusions…

"What brings you into town on a Monday afternoon?" Lindsay asked, as she handed him the mug of coffee she'd made in her single-serve brewer when she saw his truck pull into the driveway.

"I had to pick up a few things at the hardware store," he said.

Actually the trip to the store had been a ruse to explain his trip into town, but she didn't need to know that.

And though he was a little disappointed to miss seeing Avenlea—who'd gone down for a nap just before he arrived—he was glad to be able to talk to Lindsay without interruption.

"You know this isn't the hardware store, don't you?" she teased.

"I also figured, since I was in town, I'd stop by to see how you were doing," he continued, his tone as casual as his leaning-against-the-counter pose.

But maybe his tone was *too* casual, because her eyes narrowed suspiciously. "Did you think I was going to fall apart because my son went off to school this morning?"

"Again, you mean?"

He was referring, of course, to Elliott's first day of school in September, when she'd sobbed against his shoulder after her son had disappeared into the hallowed halls of kindergarten with eleven new classmates. Because yes, he'd been there, having anticipated that it would be an emotional day for Lindsay and not wanting her to have to face it alone.

"Maybe my eyes watered a little as he waved goodbye, but I did not fall apart."

"Progress," he said, nodding approvingly. "And how was Avenlea?"

"She was fine today."

Unlike that day in September, when she'd cried harder than her mom because she wanted to go to school with her beloved brother.

"But I was smarter this time," Lindsay continued. "I let her pack her backpack with some school supplies and, after her swimming lesson, we went to the library and pretended it was a classroom, because she wants to do everything Elliott does."

"I was the same with MG," Mitch said. "It's hard being the younger sibling."

"So why don't you have more sympathy for your younger sister?" she wondered.

"Because my sister is a nosy, interfering tattletale." Which didn't mean he didn't love her and wouldn't do bodily harm to anyone who ever hurt her.

Lindsay laughed softly. "You do know she's not ten years old anymore, right?"

"I know. But she's still a nosy, interfering tattletale," he said, still irritated about the observations she'd shared in the barn on New Year's Day.

"What did she do now?" she asked.

He shook his head. "It's not important."

"But now my curiosity's piqued," she said.

"She was riding MG about his Christmas present to

Paige." Which only skimmed the surface of their conversation that morning, but he figured it was enough information to satisfy Lindsay's curiosity.

"The earrings?" she guessed.

At his quizzical glance, she shrugged.

"Paige was wearing them when I ran into her at The Daily Grind last week. I commented on how pretty they were, and she said MG gave them to her."

"Well, Olivia seems to think that Paige was expecting a ring."

"I'd guess that she was probably *hoping* for a ring," Lindsay said. "But she was happy with the earrings."

"Which proves again that my sister doesn't know everything," he said.

"Just enough to get under your skin," she remarked with obvious amusement.

He waved a hand dismissively. "That's enough about Olivia. Tell me…did anything else interesting happen today?"

"Not really," she said. And then, "Ohmygod—you heard, didn't you?"

"If you're referring to your coffee date with the dad of the peanut allergy boy, then yes," he acknowledged.

"How?" she demanded. "And how do you know his son is the one with the peanut allergy? I didn't even know that."

"Caleb told me," he said.

"I'm guessing Caleb heard from Brielle," she said, naming his cousin's wife, who happened to be the kindergarten teacher. "But how did she know?"

"I'd think it's policy for teachers to be informed of potential medical issues."

She rolled her eyes. "I wasn't asking how Brielle knew about the allergy but how she heard about my plans to have coffee with Parker."

"Her TA heard it from the crossing guard who stands near the kindergarten gate."

"Sometimes I really hate this town," she muttered.

"So it's true," he said, his heart sinking as he accepted the fact. "You've got a date."

"It's *not* a date," she said. "We're meeting for coffee at ten-thirty in the morning."

"It's not the time but the intent that matters."

"Well, I don't intend to let myself be seduced over a café mocha," she told him.

"But if you were having mimosas, all bets would be off."

Her gaze narrowed.

He immediately held up his hands in a gesture of surrender. "Sorry."

"Do you have a problem with me having coffee with Parker?"

Yes.

"Of course not," he said. "I think it's great that you're getting out and meeting new people."

Thankfully, she took him at his word.

And he should have been happy for her, pleased that she was finally ready to move forward with her life after mourning the loss of her husband for more than two years. She was too young to give up on the possibility of romance, too passionate to resign herself to sleeping alone.

But the thought of her kissing another man like she'd kissed him—of another man's hands touching where his hands had touched—left him feeling decidedly *un*happy.

One of the benefits of living at the Circle G was proximity to his parents' house and the fact that they didn't mind if he stopped by at dinnertime to join them for the evening meal. In fact, he'd guess that his mom usually planned on having her whole family around the table because there was always more than enough food for everyone—plus leftovers that she'd package up for him and his brother to take back to the cabin they shared.

But he didn't eat breakfast and lunch with his parents, which meant that either he or MG had to venture into town every now and again to buy groceries. It was his turn to do the shopping this week, and he moved purposefully through the store with the list in hand until he ran into Frieda Zimmerman in the produce section, and she pulled out her phone to show him the latest video of her grandson taking his first steps. Then he spent a couple of minutes chatting with Estela Lopez, who had a big box of dog biscuits in her cart despite the fact that she'd lost her canine companion a few years earlier, because she liked to have treats on hand for the other dogs who walked through her neighborhood. He got away with exchanging waves with Deanna Raitt, a longtime server at Diggers', who was arguing with someone on her phone about the difference between Italian and French bread.

One of the things Mitch really liked about living in Haven was that neighbors looked out for one another. One of the things he disliked was that everyone knew everyone else's business. But a lot of the families who'd settled the town had been friends for generations—or, in the case of the Gilmores and Blakes, enemies. In the past few years, though, a slew of romances and reunions had brought the two families together, finally and deeply burying the hatchet on the age-old feud.

He was in the frozen food section, near the end of his list, when he noticed that his brother had scrawled an extra item on the bottom.

Oyster sauce?

What the heck was MG going to do with oyster sauce?

And where would he even find oyster sauce?

Was it a condiment? Or a seafood?

A quick Google search on his smartphone had him turning to head back to the condiments aisle when he found himself cart to cart with Heather Dekker. He and Heather had gone to school together—when her last name was Foss—and while they hadn't made an effort to keep in touch after high school graduation, it was inevitable that their paths occasionally crossed around town.

She had her little girl with her today, an adorable toddler with dark curls and big blue eyes. The child's shirt announced "I'm a Unicorn" and the sparkly crown on her head identified her as "Birthday Girl."

He remembered that she had an unusual name, but as he was completely blanking on it right now, he simply said, "I'm guessing it's someone's birthday today."

The little girl nodded enthusiastically, the movement causing the crown to slip on her baby-soft hair.

Heather adjusted the decoration on her daughter's head as she said, "Can you tell Mr. Gilmore how old you are, Silver?"

The child stretched out her arm with two fingers splayed wide.

He remembered the whispers that followed Heather's hasty marriage to James Dekker—an insurance agent at the company where she also worked. Whispers that started up again when she gave birth to a baby girl only five months later.

Mitch hadn't given it a second thought at the time. It wasn't any business of his if she was pregnant when she got married. And he didn't think anyone expected a woman to be a virgin when she exchanged her vows these days, especially one who'd been married before.

And though he wasn't judging, now that he was looking at her little girl, there was something about her...

"Two years old, huh?" he said.

Heather busied herself rearranging some items in her cart. Was she avoiding his gaze? Or simply concerned that her eggs had somehow gotten trapped beneath a bag of apples?

"Da! Da!" The little girl stretched her arms up as a man Mitch recognized as Heather's husband came down the aisle to join his family.

The dad unbuckled the belt that secured her in the cart and lifted her into his arms.

James Dekker nodded to Mitch before asking his wife, "Did you get everything on the list?"

"Everything except the ice cream," she said. "I didn't know how long it was going to take you to get the cake, and I didn't want it to melt."

"I'cweam!" Silver chimed in, clapping her hands. "I'cweam!"

"Yes, we're going to get ice cream," her mom promised.

"Ask for chocolate," Mitch said in a stage whisper to the birthday girl. "It's the best."

"If by *best* you mean *messiest*, I'd have to agree," Heather said dryly.

"I like chocolate," her husband chimed in helpfully.

As the Dekkers debated ice cream flavors, Mitch moved on in search of oyster sauce.

But as he searched the aisles, he kept picturing the little girl. And wondering why her gaze seemed disturbingly familiar.

Chapter Eight

"The big hand's almost on the three now." Elliott already had his coat and boots on, clearly impatient to be on his way to the arena. "We always leave when the big hand's on the three."

"I know," Lindsay said wearily. "But I don't think we're going to make it today."

"How come?"

"Because Avenlea's sick."

The little girl's fever seemed to come from out of nowhere. All morning she'd been her usual happy and chatty self, but by lunchtime she'd become listless and she'd barely touched the grilled cheese sandwich Lindsay had put in front of her. Afterward, she'd crawled onto the sofa with a picture book and fallen asleep. When Lindsay checked on her a few minutes later, her cheeks were flushed and warm, and a quick scan with the thermometer confirmed her fever.

Lindsay hadn't panicked. She'd been a mom long enough now to know that kids got sick—and often. But her daughter's unexpected ailment meant that Lindsay was going to have to call in reinforcements to ensure Avenlea was taken care of and Elliott made it to his weekly on-ice hockey skills session.

Two hours later, her options were exhausted and so was she. Though she had an excellent support network, it turned out that all of her usual helpers were otherwise occupied today. Arthur was at a law conference in San Diego and Suzanne had opted to go with him this trip; Gabe was at prenatal class with Kristyne; and Monica Renaldi, her next-door neighbor, had a husband currently undergoing chemotherapy treatments, and Lindsay had no idea if Avenlea's fever represented something contagious.

"It's not fair," Elliott said now. "Why do I have to miss hockey because Avenlea's sick?"

"Because I can't take her to the arena when she's running a fever," she explained patiently.

"Then Grampa can take me," he said.

"Grampa and Gramma are in San Diego and Uncle Gabe and Aunt Kristyne are busy."

"Did you call Uncle Mitch?"

"No," she admitted. "Because even if he was available to take you, by the time he drove all the way here from the Circle G, your session would be over."

"But it's skills competition day," Elliott said.

She winced, having forgotten about the monthly

competition that allowed the kids to show their coaches what they'd learned—and sent everyone home with a medal.

"I'm sorry," Lindsay said sincerely.

But her son didn't want to hear excuses or apologies.

"It's not fair," he said again, kicking the bag of equipment waiting by the front door before he stomped up the stairs to his room.

Lindsay should probably reprimand him for his behavior, except that she understood his disappointment and frustration. Unfortunately, understanding wasn't going to get him to the rink.

She checked Avenlea's temperature again, relieved to discover that the children's Advil seemed to be doing the trick and her daughter's temperature was moving in the right direction.

She heard Elliott clomping down the stairs again and exhaled a grateful sigh that he wasn't going to sulk in his room all afternoon. Maybe she'd offer to pop a bowl of corn and put on his favorite *Paw Patrol* DVD for them to watch together. It wouldn't be as much fun for him as hockey school, but she didn't think it was too bad as a consolation prize.

"Hey, El, I was thinking…" Her words trailed off when he walked into the room, holding the cordless phone out to her.

"Uncle Mitch wants to talk to you," he said.

She gave him her best "disapproving mom" look. "You called Uncle Mitch?"

"I wanna go to hockey," he said, unchastened.

Lindsay took the phone even as she made a mental

note to have a chat with her son about going behind her back later. "Hello?"

"I've already told Elliott to start getting dressed—everything but his skates. I'll be there to pick him up in fifteen minutes."

"You really don't have to come into town—"

"I was already on my way," he said.

And Elliott was already pulling equipment out of his hockey bag.

"Then I guess we'll see you in fifteen minutes," she said. "Thank you."

An hour and a half later, Mitch walked out of the arena with a sweaty—and mostly happy—little boy. But he noticed that as they drove and got closer to Winterberry Drive, Elliott's apprehension seemed to grow.

"You're worried that your mom's mad, aren't you?" he guessed.

"She *is* mad," Elliott said.

"Why do you think she's mad?"

"Because I called you without asking to use the phone," he admitted. "But if I'd asked, she would have said no."

"I don't think that's an argument in your favor," Mitch warned.

"Maybe she won't be mad if I give her my medal," Elliott said, glancing down at the silver-colored plastic disc on a ribbon around his neck.

"I think your mom will be happy to see your medal. I think she'd be even happier if you acknowledged that you were wrong to go behind her back to call me and apologized."

"But I'm not really sorry," Elliott confided. "Because if I didn't call you, I would have missed hockey."

Well, Mitch thought as he pulled into Lindsay's driveway, at least the kid was honest.

"Don't forget to hang your equipment up," he said, as he followed Elliott into the house.

"I will," the boy promised, kicking off his snow boots. "I wanna see Avenlea first."

"She's sleeping," Lindsay whispered, joining them in the foyer.

"I'll be quiet," Elliott said, hanging his coat on the child-height hook inside the closet before tiptoeing into the living room.

His sister had kicked her blanket away, so that it was hanging off the sofa. Elliott picked it up and carefully draped it over Avenlea, tucking it into the cushion behind her. Then he pulled his medal over his head and carefully placed it on the pillow beside her.

Mitch glanced at Lindsay, who was watching the scene with a small smile on her face. "How am I supposed to reprimand him now?" she asked quietly.

"You're a mom," he reminded her with a wink. "You'll figure out a way."

"I appreciate your faith in me," she said wryly. "Although, for the record, I'm not too thrilled with you right now, either."

"What did I do?" he asked, bewildered by her remark.

"You undermined my authority."

"That wasn't my intention."

"I know, but it was the result," she said. "All the parenting books I've read talk about how it's important for moms and dads to present a united front. Obviously Elliott knows that you're not his dad, but now, whenever he doesn't like what his mom says, he's going to think it's okay to ask Uncle Mitch."

The pointed reminder that he wasn't the boy's father hit its target, and she was right to call him out for overstepping. "I'm sorry."

"I'd be a lot madder if I didn't believe that," she said.

Elliott returned to the foyer then. He looked up and, catching his mom's eye, away again quickly. "I've gotta hang up my equipment."

She nodded. "Make sure you put your Under Armour in the laundry basket."

"I know."

"Just a heads-up," Mitch said to Lindsay, when Elliott had dragged his hockey bag to the laundry room to unpack it, "he wants to play real hockey next year."

"What's not real about what he does on the ice every week?" she asked.

"He means on an actual team, with practices and games."

She sighed. "I figured this was coming, but I was hoping to put it off another year."

"Why don't you want him to play on a team?"

"It's not about what I want," she said. "It's that the closest team is in Battle Mountain, and I'm not sure I can manage getting him to a practice and a game every week."

"You manage by asking for help," he told her.

"I do ask for help," she said.

"You didn't today."

"I did," she insisted. "I went through everyone on my list."

"Except me," he noted.

"Because I assumed you were at the Circle G, and by the time you drove all the way into town to pick up Elliott and then drove to the community center and got him dressed and on the ice, his session would be over."

It made sense, and yet he had to wonder: "Is that the only reason?"

"Why would you think there's another reason?" she hedged.

"Maybe because things have been awkward between us since New Year's Eve," he pointed out.

She sighed, but she didn't deny it. "I really hoped they wouldn't be."

"Obviously pretending that nothing happened isn't working," he said.

"So what are we supposed to do?" she asked warily.

He shrugged. "Maybe we should acknowledge that we're attracted to one another and, instead of dating other people, try dating each other."

And where had *that* come from?

Clearly there was a miscommunication between his brain and his mouth, because *that* was not what he'd intended to say.

But now that the words were out there, he decided that it wasn't an entirely horrible idea.

"And if it didn't work out?" Lindsay asked.

Then she shook her head before he had a chance to answer, because apparently she thought it was a horrible idea.

"I'd lose my best friend, and that's just too big a risk," she said, responding to her own question.

He took her hands in his. "You wouldn't lose me, Linds."

"How many of your ex-girlfriends do you keep in touch with?" she challenged, unconvinced.

"That's not really a fair question, because I haven't dated anyone I was friends with first."

"Because you know that dating a friend is a bad idea," she surmised.

More likely because he didn't have a lot of female friends, though he didn't admit it aloud because he didn't think it was a point in his favor.

"Anyway," he said, deciding to steer the topic of conversation back around again rather than beat his head against the wall, "hockey registration opens in a few weeks."

"I'll look into it," she promised, sounding less than enthusiastic.

"I think what you're really afraid of is that Avenlea's going to want to play, too," he said, only half teasing.

"I'm not afraid, I'm resigned," she said. "She already wants to do everything her brother does. The only reason she's not already taking skating lessons is that she's too young."

"Is that why she's in Tiny Tumblers?" he asked, referring to the introductory gymnastics program she'd been participating in for the past several months.

"That and I needed her to have a safe outlet for all her energy so that she's not bouncing on the furniture. But she'll have to miss it tomorrow," Lindsay realized. "Although she seems to have rebounded, I think we'll stay home—just to be safe.

"I talked to my mom when you were at the rink," she continued. "And she thinks Avenlea might finally be getting her second molars—which is the first thing I should have considered when I saw her red cheeks."

"The important thing is that she's rebounded," Mitch said. "And that Elliott didn't miss hockey."

"I still feel as if I should ground him for using the phone without permission."

"If he'd asked, would you have said yes?"

"No. For the same reasons that I gave him when he asked if I'd called you." She closed her eyes and exhaled a weary sigh. "I hate having to be the bad guy all the time."

"You're not the bad guy," he assured her. "You're a single parent doing the best that you can—which, by the way, is a pretty awesome job from my perspective."

Lindsay managed a smile. "I'm not sure my kids would agree with that, but thank you for saying so."

And then, in an obvious effort to shift the topic of conversation, she asked, "So why were you on your way into town when Elliott called?"

"Oh, crap." Mitch glanced at the time displayed on his phone. "I was supposed to do a favor for someone."

"Did you at least call to tell her that you were going to be late?"

He frowned. "I never said the someone was a her."

"You also never gave a name, which you would have done if it was a him."

"You're right," he acknowledged. "The someone is Brittney who, incidentally, I dated for several months last year and yet somehow managed to maintain a friendly relationship."

"And what's the favor you're supposed to do for Brittney?" she asked curiously.

"She's having trouble with a closet door sticking and asked if I could take a look at it."

"Bedroom closet?" Lindsay guessed.

"I have no idea."

"And no clue."

"What's that supposed to mean?"

"Your *friend* Brittney wants to get back together."

"No, she doesn't."

"The stuck closet door is totally a ploy to get you over to her place so that she can get you into bed."

"Well, that's not happening," he said.

And then it was his turn to signal a topic of conversation was closed, which he did by asking, "How was your coffee date last week?"

She feigned shock at the question. "You mean you didn't get all the details from the barista's cousin's best friend's sister?"

"She was surprisingly tight-lipped about the encounter," he said, his own lips twitching as he fought against a smile.

"Or maybe there wasn't much to say," Lindsay said.

"Was it just coffee? Or did you go wild and have a doughnut, too?"

"Just coffee," she said. "Actually, I had a café mocha, so I guess I went partially wild. Parker had regular coffee and a chocolate peanut butter banana croissant."

"So…are you going to see him again?"

She nodded. "We're meeting for coffee again in a couple of weeks."

"Coffee again?" he asked, surprised—and secretly relieved. "I guess that means there were no sparks, huh?"

"Why would you say that?"

"Because if there were sparks, you'd be progressing from coffee to dinner—or at least lunch," he said.

"We had a very pleasant conversation," she said, a little defensively. "And anyway, sparks are overrated."

"Which isn't at all what you'd be saying if there were sparks."

"Maybe you're right," she said. "But the fact is, there's only one guy who ever made my heart race with just a look."

"Nathan." He winced, feeling suddenly guilty for teasing her.

But she surprised him by shaking her head. "No. Don't get me wrong—I loved Nathan with my whole heart, but the attraction between us took a while to develop."

"Then who?" he asked.

She shook her head again, refusing to meet his gaze. "Forget I said anything."

"You can't say something like that and expect me to not want to know," he chided.

"Well, I'm not going to tell you."

"Why…" His words trailed off as an unlikely possibility teased his mind. "Wait a minute—was it me?"

"It was a long time ago," she said, her cheeks turning pink.

"It was me," he realized, stunned.

"I was fifteen," she said, a little defensively, "with all those teenage hormones running rampant through my system, and we spent a lot of time together that summer."

"We spent a lot of time together in almost every season."

"Thankfully puberty wasn't an issue every season."

"So…that summer," he prompted.

The color in her cheeks deepened. "I can't believe I'm telling you this."

"You haven't really told me anything yet," he pointed out to her.

"We were sitting shoulder to shoulder in the movie theater, sharing a tub of popcorn…and you smelled so good…and when you leaned down to whisper something to me, the warmth of your breath on my ear sent sparks dancing in my veins."

"It was *Spider-Man*," he said, proving that his memory of that day was as clear as hers. "The first Tobey Maguire one."

She nodded.

"I'd just gotten my license and had to beg to borrow my dad's truck to drive into town to pick you up." She'd been wearing low-rise jeans with a cropped top, so that a couple inches of tanned midriff were exposed, with gold hoop earrings and shiny gloss on her lips.

"And my mom insisted that we take Kristyne with us, because she wanted to see the movie, too," Lindsay said.

"But you wouldn't let her sit with us, so she sat two rows back and threw popcorn at us."

She smiled at the memory. "Good times."

"I wish I'd known that you felt sparks," he said.

"It was a long time ago—and the feeling was obviously one-sided."

"Why would you say that?"

"Because only a few months later, when I told you that Nathan had invited me to go to the prom with him, you said that I should accept his invitation."

"What was I supposed to say?" he demanded. "Should I have told you that Nathan knew I was planning to ask you and he asked first, because everything was always a competition with Nathan?"

Her jaw actually dropped open at this revelation, but she pulled it up again to respond. "You were going to ask me to the prom?"

"And that was a secret I'd planned to take to my grave," he said, then immediately winced at the insensitive phrasing. "I'm sorry. I didn't mean it that way."

She winced, too, but then she drew in a breath and fluttered her fingers, waving off his apology. "You were going to ask me to the prom?" she said again, determined to get an answer to the question.

"Yes," he finally admitted.

And he'd told Nate—in strict confidence—about his plan, because he thought his friend, who already had something of a reputation as a ladies' man, might have some advice for him.

"My advice is to ask someone else," Nate said.

"Why not Lindsay?"

"Because you don't have a hope in hell of getting past first base with Lindsay. And why would you spend two hundred bucks on prom tickets unless you think there's a chance you'll get to see what your date's wearing under her dress?"

"Because I like her," he said, unwilling to be dissuaded.

Nate shrugged. "I'm probably going to take Heather, even though we've already done it a few times."

Which Mitch knew, because Nate boasted about it every time it happened.

"But…why didn't you?" Lindsay asked, seemingly baffled by his reticence. "You had to know I would never say no to you."

"But I didn't want you to say yes because it was an invitation from a friend—I wanted you to say yes because you wanted to go with me as much as I wanted to go with you. Because you felt about me the way I felt about you."

"How did you feel about me?"

"I liked you. A lot."

"I had no idea," she admitted.

"I didn't want you to know," he said. "I didn't want our relationship to get weird."

"You mean like now?"

He managed a wry smile. "Yeah. And anyway, I was sure the crush would fade away if I just ignored it."

"Obviously it did," she said.

"Eventually," he agreed. "But when you kissed me on

New Year's Eve, it was like the realization of a dream I've had since I was fifteen years old."

"I'm glad I didn't know that beforehand," she said lightly. "That kind of pressure might have been intimidating."

She was joking, of course, steering them back to familiar ground where they were friends with a long history that he now knew included some surprising feelings on both sides.

But they'd both moved on from those feelings a long time ago, and he'd be a fool to acknowledge that one kiss had stirred up his desire again.

"This is a nice surprise," Lindsay said, opening the door for her sister the following Saturday morning.

"I brought treats," Kristyne said, holding up the box from Sweet Caroline's.

"Another nice surprise." She looked past her sister. "Where's Gabe?"

"Closed up in his music room at home. Practicing for his upcoming studio session."

"Does he know you left the house?"

"I didn't sneak out," Kristyne said dryly.

"Well, the way he's been hovering like a hummingbird at a feeder since your last doctor's appointment, I thought I should ask."

"And I had another appointment this week and the doctor assured us both that everything is fine," her sister told her.

While Kristyne was hanging up her coat, Lindsay

called into the family room to Elliott and Avenlea to let them know their aunt was there—with treats.

"Auntiekwisty!" Avenlea called out, racing to greet her beloved aunt. After a quick hug, she drew back and gently patted Kristyne's round belly. "Hi, Baby."

"Baby says hi back," the expectant mom told her.

Avenlea giggled. "Baby can't talk."

"Right here," Kristyne said, moving her niece's hand to the side. "Do you feel that?"

The little girl nodded, her eyes wide.

"That's the baby's way of saying hi."

Avenlea still wasn't entirely convinced. "We-wy?"

"Uh-huh. Of course the baby's favorite time to chat is three o'clock in the morning. Or when I've got a full bladder—which seems like always these days."

"You bwin' tweats?" Avenlea asked, proving that her interest in the baby wasn't as keen as her sweet tooth.

Elliott had bypassed his aunt completely in favor of the bakery box on the table—until he caught his mother's eye.

"Thanks for the treats, Aunt Kristyne."

"You're welcome," she said. "But you have to save some for your sister and your mom and me."

"An' me," Avenlea piped up.

"You're the sister," Elliott told her, adding a dramatic eye roll to express his exasperation.

"Oh."

"I'm a sister, too," Kristyne said, as Lindsay poured milk for the kids.

Elliott appeared skeptical of this information. "You're our aunt."

"Because I'm your mom's sister—and she's mine."

The little boy still looked perplexed as he bit into a jelly-filled doughnut.

"We'll sort out the family tree next week," Lindsay promised.

When Elliott and Avenlea had finished their snack and had their hands and faces washed, Lindsay sent them off to play so that she and Kristyne could chat over cups of chai tea that she'd brewed.

"You mentioned a doctor's appointment this week," she said, sitting down across from her sister. "Did you have another ultrasound?"

"I did."

Lindsay surveyed the contents of the box, trying to decide between a lemon meringue tart and Boston cream doughnut. "Boy or girl?"

"Not telling," Kristyne said.

Knowing that her sister had a fondness for Boston cream and because there was only one in the box, Lindsay opted for the tart.

"Because you don't know," she deduced. "If you did, you wouldn't be able to keep it to yourself."

"You're right," her sister admitted. "And I thought I wanted to know, but at the last minute, when the tech was ready to tell us, I said no. Which is silly, right?"

"Why is it silly? Lots of expectant parents prefer to wait until delivery to find out."

"I just think it would be so much easier to prepare if we knew."

"You *are* prepared," Lindsay reminded her. "The nursery is painted, the furniture is in place, the dresser is filled with diapers and onesies and sleepers—and I've got plenty of newborn clothes for boys *and* girls, ready to go as soon as you tell me what you need."

"You're right," Kristyne said. "I think it's the name that's the problem. I'm tired of referring to my baby as 'him or her' or 'he or she.' I want to be able to say Jack or Jill."

"I gave you a book with more than ten thousand baby names and those are your options?"

Her sister laughed. "No, they're just random examples. Although Jack is on our short list of boys' names."

"Dad would love that," Lindsay said.

Kristyne absently rubbed a hand over her belly as she nibbled on the Boston cream.

"Why do I get the feeling there's more on your mind than baby names?" Lindsay asked.

"I'm a little worried about Gabe's upcoming trip to LA," her sister admitted. "And that he might not be here when I go into labor."

Lindsay was worried, too, though probably for different reasons. But there was no way she was going to add her concerns to those already weighing on Kristyne's mind. "His trip is next week, isn't it?"

"It's been bumped back two more weeks," her sister said.

Which meant two weeks closer—and now very close—to Kristyne's due date.

"You don't have to worry," Lindsay said confidently, even as she crossed her fingers under the table and said a quick and silent prayer that her sister's husband would return on time and, more important, safely. "He'll be back."

"How do you know?"

"Because there's no way he's not going to be there to help bring your baby into the world," she promised.

And because—the crash that killed Nathan notwithstanding—flying was the safest mode of transportation.

"Plus, and I know you don't want to hear this," Lindsay continued, "but first babies are almost always late."

"Yeah," Kristyne rubbed a hand over her round belly. "I definitely don't want to hear that."

"Elliott didn't come until a full week after my due date," she said, choosing to focus on the labor process rather than her brother-in-law's travel.

"That does make me feel a little bit better about Gabe's trip—and a little bit like this pregnancy is going to go on forever. But just in case…would you be my backup labor coach?"

"I'll give you all my Boston cream doughnuts forever if I get to be there when my first niece or nephew is born," Lindsay promised.

And added a silent vow to be there for her sister always, no matter what.

Chapter Nine

Lindsay was setting up for the Toddlers and Tots story time, positioning thick, colorful pillows in a semicircle on the floor facing the storyteller's throne—an old red velvet wing chair that someone had donated to the library long before she started working there. Quinn, hanging out at the library as she was in the habit of doing when she was struggling with her writing, had wandered over to the adult section to browse the stacks when Lindsay began checking in parents and children for story time Wednesday morning.

Reading aloud and sharing her love of stories with little ones was one of her favorite parts of the job. An added bonus was that she got to meet a lot of parents and the young children who would go to school with Elliott and Avenlea.

"Heather Foss." She smiled, genuinely happy to see the classmate she'd lost touch with a lot of years earlier, even before she and Nathan had moved away. But she would have recognized Heather anywhere, because the woman looked just as fabulous as she had ten years earlier. Her platinum-blond hair was shorter now and there were laugh lines at the corners of her eyes and mouth that hadn't been there a decade and a half earlier, but otherwise she looked the same. "It's great to see you. How are you doing?"

The other woman's answering smile was thin. "It's Heather Dekker now."

Lindsay winced inwardly at the faux pas even as she nodded. "Of course. I saw your name on the story-time registration." She scanned the list on her tablet again and tapped to check the attendance box. "Here you are—Heather and Silver. Oh, that's a beautiful and unique name."

"Thank you. It's something of a family name… on her dad's side," Heather said.

Lindsay turned her attention to the little girl clinging tightly to her mother's hand. "Welcome to story time, Silver."

The child offered a shy smile even as she ducked her head a little.

"How long have you worked here?" Heather asked.

"I just started in the fall. Part-time," Lindsay explained. "Tuesday and Thursday mornings, full days on Wednesdays and one Saturday a month. It's a great schedule, because I can take Elliott to school in the morning and pick him up again at the end of the day, and it means Avenlea only has to be in day care part-time."

"You have two kids?"

She nodded. "How about you?"

"Just Silver for now," she said, loosening up enough to smile down at her daughter. "But she's going to be a big sister in about six and a half months."

"Congratulations," Lindsay said sincerely.

"Thanks." Heather hesitated briefly then before saying, "I should have reached out when I heard about Nathan's passing…to tell you that I was sorry for your loss."

It was what most people said when she saw them for the first time after her husband's passing. And in the early days, the words had always hit her like a sucker punch to the gut, knocking the air out of her lungs and making her knees want to buckle. But with each day that passed, the grief faded a little more and she got a little stronger. Now the words caused no more than a slight twinge—bittersweet proof that she was healing.

"Thank you," she said.

"It can't be easy, raising your children without a dad," Heather acknowledged hesitantly.

"It's the reason we came back to Haven," she confided. "Because Nate's parents are here, and my sister and her husband, and Mitchell, of course."

"You and Mitch are still friends?"

Lindsay nodded.

"That's good," Heather said, though her tone was dubious. "Well…we should go find a place on the carpet."

"And quick, before it's standing room only," Lindsay said, obviously joking.

Heather offered another thin smile before moving toward the circle with her daughter.

"That was weird," Quinn remarked, as Heather and Silver went to join the group of moms and toddlers already seated in a semicircle facing the storyteller's throne.

"You thought so, too?" Lindsay said.

Her friend nodded. "You two have some kind of history?"

"We went through school together," Lindsay acknowledged. "But before today, I hadn't seen her in… I couldn't even tell you how many years."

"Friends who lost touch?"

"We didn't hang out together, but we weren't *not* friends," she said. "In fact, she dated my husband— a long time before he was my husband."

"Did you steal her from him?" Quinn asked, only half teasing.

"Of course not!" she immediately denied.

"Then why are you frowning?"

Lindsay deliberately relaxed her facial muscles, smoothing her brow. "I guess I did date him right after he broke up with Heather," she acknowledged. "But that was more than sixteen years ago."

"Some people know how to hold a grudge," her friend noted.

Lindsay shook her head. "It's not as if Nathan broke her heart. In fact, she tied the knot with some guy she met at college before me and Nate got married. Actually, I think she might have been separated—or maybe even divorced—before our wedding.

"Her current husband, James Dekker, is her third. And it's a third marriage for him, too. But they say the third time's the charm."

"Who's they?" Quinn wondered aloud. "And how is it that you were gone for more than five years and you still know what's going on with everyone in this town before I do?"

"I stop at The Daily Grind every morning before work," she explained.

"Where the coffee is hot and the gossip is hotter," her friend acknowledged.

"See what you miss out on when you get your java from Sweet Caroline's instead?"

"You're the one missing out. Sweet Caroline's pastries put The Daily Grind to shame."

"Obviously, you haven't had the s'mores muffin from the coffee shop," Lindsay told her.

"There's no way it can compare to the chocolate peanut butter banana croissant at the bakery."

"That's what Parker had when we met for coffee—he said they're addictive."

"They are," Quinn confirmed. "I can't walk past Sweet Caroline's without popping in to get one. Or two. Because even a day old, they're delicious."

"Enough talk about muffins and croissants," Lindsay said. "My stomach is starting to rumble and it's still two hours until my lunch break."

"Did you brown bag it today?"

She nodded. "But I didn't pack anything that won't

keep until tomorrow, if you were planning to stick around."

"I've got some research to do," Quinn said. "And I've been craving a Diggers' buffalo chicken wrap with spicy fries."

"Go do your research and stop making me think about food," Lindsay said, shooing her friend.

Quinn started to go, then paused to ask, "What story are you reading today?"

She glanced at the book on top of the desk and sighed. *"The Very Hungry Caterpillar."*

Her friend walked away laughing.

When Elliott was promoted from "hockey skills" to "hockey school," his sessions changed from Saturday afternoons to mornings. Lindsay had not been thrilled with the new time slot, and Avenlea was even less so—a fact that was evident to Mitch when he joined the mom and daughter watching the activity on the ice.

"Someone looks like a grumpy pants this morning," he remarked, as he lowered himself onto the seat beside Lindsay.

"Early mornings in a cold arena are not my idea of fun," she told him.

He chuckled. "Actually, I was referring to your daughter."

"Hers, either," she acknowledged.

But the little girl had spotted "Uncamitch" and was already crawling across her mom's lap to get to him.

She eyed the tray of to-go cups in his hand with

wide eyes. "Did you bwin' hot choc'ate, Uncamitch?" she asked hopefully.

"You know I did," he said.

He pried the small cup out of the tray and removed the stirrer from the opening in the domed lid so that she could sip from it.

"Half hot chocolate, half cold milk," he told Lindsay, so that she wouldn't worry about her daughter burning her mouth.

"What do you say to Uncle Mitch?" Lindsay prompted.

"I wuv you, Uncamitch."

Lindsay laughed softly. "Try 'thank you, Uncle Mitch.'"

"Thank you, Uncamitch," the little girl dutifully intoned.

"Thank you, Uncle Mitch," Lindsay echoed, as he handed her a large cup of hot coffee.

She took her first sip, then sighed with blissful pleasure. "Café mocha," she realized. "What did I do to deserve this?"

He shrugged. "I know how much you hate early mornings in a cold arena."

"You really are the best," she told him.

"That's what all the women say," he said with a wink.

She nudged him with her elbow, a little harder than would be considered playful, making him grunt as she connected with his ribs.

"You had your chance to be one of those women and you turned it down," he reminded her.

"Speaking of those women—did you ever get over to fix Brittney's closet?"

"No," he admitted. "Apparently Brett Tanner is fixing her doors these days."

"So I was right," she said triumphantly.

He shrugged. "Since I never made it over to her place that night, I guess we'll never know."

"You know," she said. "You just don't want to admit it."

Instead of confirming or denying, he turned his attention to the kids on the ice, picking Elliott out of the crowd right away. "His skating is really coming along," he noted.

"He's making progress," she acknowledged. "But he's not very intuitive on the ice."

"Does he have fun?" Mitch asked.

"He loves it."

"Then that's all that matters."

"You're right," she said. "It's just…"

"It's just what?"

She sighed. "Nathan would get so frustrated with him. He had Elliott on the ice as soon as he was big enough for skates, determined to make his son into an even better hockey player than he'd been. But it doesn't come naturally to Elliott."

"Nate was pretty serious about hockey…until he discovered girls—I mean *you*," Mitch quickly amended.

"You don't have to revise history on my account," she told him. "I was there. I know he earned his reputation."

Which was only one of the reasons Mitch had been concerned when Nate and Lindsay first hooked up. He'd been certain that Lindsay would end up with her heart broken if she was foolish enough to fall in love with Nate. He'd never anticipated that Nate would fall first.

"Since you brought up the subject of Nathan's past," Lindsay began.

"Did I?" he asked warily.

"Something strange happened at the library the other day," she continued.

"What's that?"

"Heather Foss—now Heather Dekker—came in for story time with her daughter."

"Why is that strange?" He kept his tone casual, ignoring the uneasiness that skittered down his spine.

"The strange part is the way she acted," Lindsay said. "I know we were never the best of friends, but we were friendly. And at the library, she really wasn't."

"You're probably reading something into nothing," he said.

"I don't know…even Quinn remarked that it was odd."

"It's Quinn's job to make stuff up," he reminded her.

"One of the reasons she's such a good writer is that she has keen observation skills," Lindsay pointed out. "Anyway, she asked if I stole Nathan from Heather in high school, which got me wondering if maybe I did."

He laughed. "Are you seriously worried about something that happened sixteen years ago?"

"Did I steal Nathan from Heather?" she pressed.

"No," he said. "At least, not on purpose."

She frowned at that. "Are you saying that I *accidentally* stole him?"

"I'm saying that Nate wasn't the type of guy to let

obstacles stand in his way, and when he decided that he wanted to go out with you, he dumped Heather.

"But I can't imagine that she's still holding a grudge over that," he was quick to assure her, when he saw the stricken expression on her face. "It's more likely that she was just having an off day."

"Maybe," Lindsay allowed. "And speaking of off days…how did you wrangle the day off?"

"MG owed me a favor."

"And you called it in so that you could drive into town to sit in a cold arena on a Saturday morning?"

"It beats sitting in a cold saddle with the icy wind in my face riding fence in the back forty," he told her.

"I guess it's all a matter of perspective, isn't it?" she mused. "Anyway, we're heading to The Trading Post when Elliott gets off the ice. He asked if I would make lasagna this weekend, so that's our plan for dinner tonight, if you want to join us."

"That sounds great, but I've actually got plans tonight," he said. "Any chance you can save the lasagna for tomorrow?"

"Wait," she said, holding up a hand. "You skipped over the mention of plans really fast…do you have a date tonight?"

"I'd rather not put a label on it, but that one probably fits," he admitted.

Lindsay knew that she should be happy for him. A good friend would be pleased to hear that he'd met someone he was interested in pursuing a relationship with. A good friend would want to hear all about his plans and eventually even meet the object of his affection.

And if she wasn't actually happy about his news—and she'd think about the reasons for that later—the least she could do was fake it.

"That's great," she said brightly. "What's her name? Where'd you meet her?"

"Her name's Sheridan, and I'm meeting her at Diggers' tonight," he said, sounding less than enthused by the prospect.

"A blind date," she noted, surprised.

"Sort of." He shrugged. "She's a friend of Paige's, so MG and Paige and me and Sheridan are having dinner together."

"Well…that's great," she said again.

"Maybe you should say *great* a third time to convince me," he suggested in a dry tone.

"Sorry," she said. "I was just caught off guard. But it *is* great, because you're a terrific guy and you deserve to share your life with someone special."

"It's just dinner," he said dismissively.

"Every relationship has to start somewhere," she pointed out.

"So does tomorrow night work for the lasagna instead?" he prompted.

"Sure," she agreed. "But why don't we confirm in the morning? Just in case."

"In case of what?"

Was he really that obtuse?

"In case you really hit it off with Sheridan and want to see her again tomorrow night," she explained.

He shook his head. "Even if we did hit it off, that kind of eagerness screams of desperation," he told her. "I'm a firm believer in waiting at least three days after a date to reach out."

"And while you're waiting three days, she might be getting a dozen hits from Tinder or Bumble or OkCupid and decide to move on without you," Lindsay said, not sure if her words were intended as a warning to him or reassurance to herself.

"Why would she agree to have dinner with me if she's looking for someone through online dating sites?" Mitchell asked, sounding more curious than concerned.

"Because she's a woman who wants to be in a relationship and Haven isn't exactly a booming metropolis?" Lindsay suggested.

Instead of arguing the point he asked, "How do you know so much about online dating?"

"My world might revolve around my children, but I get out and talk to people," she said.

"By people you mean Quinn," he guessed.

She sighed. "Is my world really that small?"

"It's hardly a booming metropolis," he said, teasing her with her own words.

"My point is, if you have a good time tonight, you should give her a call tomorrow…unless you wake up with her, in which case a phone call probably won't be necessary—and might even be weird."

"This conversation is weird," he decided.

"It shouldn't be," she said, though she couldn't deny that it was. "Didn't we promise one another that we wouldn't let things be weird?"

"It's not weird because I'm discussing my dating prospects with you after what happened on New Year's Eve," he told her. "It's weird because it's not something I'd usually discuss with *anyone*."

"Not even your brother or one of your buddies?"

"No," he said firmly.

"How did this double date get set up if you didn't talk to MG about it?" she challenged.

"He said, 'You got any plans for Saturday night?' I said, 'No.' He said, 'Paige has a friend she wants you to meet.' I said, *'Hell, no.'* He said, 'I've been told to make sure you're there, so I need you to be there.' And I said, 'Okay.'"

"You didn't ask any questions about Paige's friend?" she asked incredulously.

He shrugged again. "I figured I'd learn everything I need to know when we're at dinner."

"Do you at least know her last name, so you can check out her social media?"

"No. And even if I did, I wouldn't tell you, because I don't want *you* checking out her social media or— worse—making contact with her."

"I wouldn't do that," she protested.

He gave her a look.

"Probably not," she amended, as the kids on the ice, exhausted from their workout, funneled toward the open door to retreat to their dressing rooms. "But you can't blame me for looking out for you."

"I can look out for myself," he assured her.

She shook her head. "You don't realize what a catch you are."

His brows lifted then. "You think I'm a catch?"

"We're not talking about me—we're talking about Paige's friend with the baited hook."

"Here's a better idea—" he rose from his seat "—let's stop talking about this altogether."

"Where are you going?"

"To help Elliott with his skates and equipment," Mitchell said, and made his escape.

"I didn't expect to have to share the TV with you tonight," Mitch remarked, carrying two bottles of beer into the living room where his brother was already settled on the sofa with a game on TV the following Friday night.

"I do still live here," MG told him.

"Do you? I wasn't sure."

"Ha ha." He accepted the bottle of beer his brother offered. "You know I never spend more than two consecutive nights at Paige's place."

"Why is that?" Mitch wondered, twisting the cap off his own bottle.

"Because I don't want her to start to think that we're living together."

"Because that would be a bigger commitment than you're willing to make."

"It's a slippery slope," MG noted. "Although, unlike you, I can at least commit to a second date."

"You're talking about Sheridan," he guessed.

"You been on any other first dates lately?"

"Not lately."

"She told Paige that she really liked you."

"I think her opinion changed dramatically when Paige told her that the Circle G is one of the biggest cattle ranches in Nevada."

"So?"

"So there was no real chemistry between us."

"Sometimes it's hard to gauge chemistry across a dinner table—especially when there are two other people there."

"I'm not interested," Mitch said bluntly.

MG shrugged. "Okay, then."

"You're not going to try to maneuver us together again?" he asked, wary of his brother's easy acquiescence.

"I promised Paige that I'd get you to the restaurant. I didn't promise that you'd hit it off with her friend," MG said.

"Okay, then," Mitch echoed, and tipped his bottle to his lips again.

They watched the game in silence for several minutes before MG said, "Something else is on your mind."

"What?"

"Vegas just scored a short-handed goal and you didn't even blink, so I figured your mind must be on something other than the game."

"Yeah," Mitch admitted.

But he wasn't sure if he should say anything more than that. He wasn't even sure there was anything to say.

Over the past month, he'd tried to ignore the alarms that clanged in his head whenever he thought about the encounter with Heather at The Trading Post. But since Lindsay had shared the details of her interaction with

Heather at the library, those alarms had been harder to ignore.

"Good talk," MG said, after a long moment had passed without his brother elaborating on his single word response.

Mitch managed a wry smile. "Did you ever find yourself in a position of knowing something that you didn't want to know?"

"Sometimes ignorance is bliss," his brother agreed.

He nodded and swallowed another mouthful of beer.

"Does this have something to do with Lindsay?" MG asked.

"Why would you think that?"

"Because anytime you get twisted up over something, it has to do with Lindsay."

"Actually, it's about Nathan," he said.

"Who was Lindsay's husband," his brother pointed out.

As if he might have forgotten.

After another minute passed, MG asked, "Did he cheat on her?"

Mitch frowned at the question. "That came from out in left field."

"Hardly," his brother scoffed. "The guy was a total player before Lindsay."

"But he changed when he fell for her," he felt compelled to point out. And it might have surprised Mitch, but there was no denying it was true.

"Maybe," his brother said dubiously.

"What do you know that I don't?"

"I don't *know* anything," MG denied. "But I did see

Nate at Diggers' that weekend he was home for his mom's birthday."

"And?" Mitch prompted.

"He was with Heather Foss. Or Dekker. Or whatever her name was at the time. And they were all over each other at the bar."

"You never told me that," Mitch said, surprised by his brother's silence then more than his revelation now.

MG slowly curled his hand into a fist and stared at his knuckles. "I didn't tell you because I didn't want to have to bail you out of jail after you beat him to a bloody pulp. I figured the fat lip I gave him made the same point but without the necessity of a police presence."

"You got in a fight with Nate at Diggers'?"

"It was outside," MG said. "You know Duke has a strict rule about fighting in the bar. And it wasn't a fight—I hit him once but he never hit back, probably because he knew he deserved it."

"You're right, I would have beat him bloody," Mitch said.

"And I would have bailed you out, but I'm glad I didn't have to."

"The question now is—do I tell Lindsay?"

"She won't thank you if you do," MG cautioned.

"I know," he agreed. "It just seems like a really big secret to keep."

"And a really big secret to tell."

Mitch swallowed his last mouthful of beer.

"Nate's gone—all she's got left are her memories, and if you tell her that he picked up with his ex-girlfriend when he was in town, all those shiny, happy memories will be tarnished forever."

And maybe, if that's all that had happened, Mitch might have been able to let it go.

"Heather's little girl turned two in January," he told his brother.

MG considered this for a beat, then swore, proving that he could do the math and knew what the answer was when two-plus-two equaled a baby nine months later. "So possibly a bigger secret than I realized."

"Do you still think I shouldn't tell her?" Mitch asked.

"I think that once the words are spoken, they can't be taken back."

"But if she hears about it from someone else and later finds out that I knew and didn't tell her, she might never forgive me."

MG lifted his beer as if offering a toast. "Welcome to the space known as 'between a rock and a hard place.'"

"I need a spa day," Quinn announced, dropping a stack of books on the checkout counter.

"Deadline crunch?" Lindsay guessed, as she began scanning the items.

"Am I that predictable?"

"You do tend to get stressed when you have a book due," she told her friend.

"In six weeks," Quinn said. "I only have six weeks to wrap up the story and catch the bad guy."

"And you'll do it," Lindsay said confidently, because Quinn's ability to deliver was as dependable as her panic. "But if you need some extra incentive to push through, make an appointment at Serenity Spa for the day after your manuscript is due as your reward."

"That's a good plan," Quinn agreed, scrolling through the calendar app on her phone. "Is April second good for you? It's a Friday—and you're off Fridays, right?"

"I don't work here on Fridays," she agreed. "But I still have two kids that need to be taken care of—and only one is in school during the day."

"I'm sure your mother-in-law would be happy to spend a few hours with Avenlea."

"She would, but I'm not the one who needs a spa day," Lindsay pointed out.

"You have two kids," Quinn said, echoing her words. "You probably need a spa day as much as I do."

The idea was certainly tempting. "Well, I wouldn't mind a pedicure," Lindsay said, as she finished scanning the books. "And I've got a gift certificate." Actually, she had two of them, because Suzanne and Arthur had given them to her for her birthday the past couple of years.

"Mark it in your calendar," Quinn said. "April second—spa day."

Lindsay did as directed and realized that she was sincerely looking forward to an afternoon of relaxation and fun with a girlfriend—yet more proof that life did go on.

Chapter Ten

After his blind date with Sheridan had turned out to be a dud, Mitch didn't know why he let his sister talk him into agreeing to another setup—this time with a woman who'd recently joined the same yoga studio. Olivia had not only insisted that he meet Karli but that he take her somewhere nice, so he'd made a reservation at The Home Station, the only upscale restaurant in town.

Karli was as attractive as his sister had promised, with auburn hair and whiskey-colored eyes and a sprinkle of freckles across her nose. She was also tall—probably close to six feet in the high-heeled boots she wore with a dark purple sweater dress. And smart, with a civil engineering degree with specialization in environmental and water issues from Northwestern Michigan College.

"How did you end up in Haven?" he wondered.

"I came to town to do an environmental assessment for Blake Mining."

"So it's a short-term assignment?"

"I thought so," she said. "But there's the possibility of it becoming a permanent position, if they're happy with my work and if I want to stay." She smiled at him then. "And I've seen a lot to like about this town so far."

The date seemed to be off to a promising start when a short chirp sounded from his phone.

"Sorry." He reached into his pocket for the offending device. "Just let me turn off my notifications so…"

His words trailed off when he saw the message.

Kristyne's in labor and Gabe's in LA.

The unasked question from Lindsay was, could he watch Elliott and Avenlea so that she could go to the hospital with her sister, as they'd previously discussed?

He immediately replied:

Be there in 10.

"Is something wrong?" Karli asked.

"I'm sorry," he said. "I have to go. The sister of a friend of mine is having a baby, and I promised I'd watch her kids so that she could coach her through labor."

"I like kids," Karli said. "I'd be happy to babysit with you."

While Lindsay had seemed cool about him dating,

he was pretty sure she wouldn't approve of him bringing a woman he'd just met into her home to help take care of Elliott and Avenlea. Truthfully, he wasn't comfortable with that scenario, either.

"Thanks, but you should stay and order dinner," he said, already pushing his chair back from the table. "The food here is really good, and I'll leave my credit card with the maître d' to cover the check."

And then, without waiting for her to respond, he was gone.

"That was quick," Lindsay said, when she opened the door in response to his knock.

"I told you I'd be here in ten."

"And you made it with—" she glanced at her watch "—just about thirty seconds to spare."

He lifted his brows when he heard a beep from the kitchen. "Were you timing me?"

She laughed. "No. That's the oven signaling that it's preheated. We were late getting home from the children's museum in Battle Mountain and I was just about to put chicken fingers in for the kids' dinner."

She turned toward the kitchen, but he caught her shoulders and steered her back around again.

"Your sister's waiting for you," he reminded her.

"I know, but—"

"Auntiekwisty's havin' a baby!" Drawn away from her toys by the sound of their voices, Avenlea bounced into the foyer to make the announcement.

"I hope it's a boy," Elliott said, joining them.

"Giwl!" Avenlea countered.

"Boy or girl, your aunt Kristyne will be having her baby at home if your mom doesn't leave right now," Mitch said.

Lindsay swallowed. "You're right. I have to go. Just let me—"

"You've got your keys and your purse," he noted. "That's all you need. I can handle things here."

"I know," she said again, bending to give her children a quick hug. "Thank you."

So while Lindsay headed back to Battle Mountain, to the hospital with her sister this time, Mitch cooked the chicken fingers. He even cut carrot sticks and cucumber slices to go with them, because Lindsay believed it was important for the kids to have vegetables at every meal. And because he knew Elliott and Avenlea liked to dip, he squirted little pools of barbecue sauce and ranch dressing on their plates.

When it was time to eat, Avenlea's previously discerning palate proved that it was either confused or adventurous, because she chose to dip her chicken in the ranch dressing and her cucumber in the barbecue sauce. Of course, this caused her brother to make gagging noises, but Mitch quickly silenced Elliott's criticism, pointing out that everything was going to the same place.

It was what his mom had always said, insisting that as long as kids were eating—and what they were eating wasn't harmful to them—there was no reason to worry about unconventional food choices. No doubt that was why leftover pizza was still one of Mitch's favorite breakfast foods.

After dinner was finished, he enlisted Elliott and Avenlea to help clear the table and put their plates and cups in the dishwasher. Then they washed up and got their pajamas on, ready for bed.

"But we don't have to go to bed right now, do we?" Elliott asked.

"Not right now," Mitch agreed.

Though he'd forgotten to verify bedtimes with Lindsay before she left, he didn't think it would be a big deal if they were a little bit later for one night. And yes, he could have sent her a text message to ask, but he didn't want to take her focus away from her sister.

She'd checked in with him, though, when they got to the hospital, and again to tell him that Kristyne was four centimeters dilated. He didn't know if that was good or bad and, truthfully, he didn't want to think about it too much. He couldn't be a rancher if he was squeamish about the process of birth, and he'd witnessed more calves and foals being born than he could possibly remember—and even a couple litters of kittens. But baby cows and horses came when they were ready, and it was most often a completely natural process. Human beings tended to make everything more complicated, and Mitch preferred not to think about the details of Lindsay's sister expelling a baby from her birth canal.

Of course, as soon as he'd decided not to worry about strict adherence to the children's usual nighttime schedule, his phone chirped with another message.

Bedtime is 7 for Avenlea and 8 for Elliott (usually) ;)

He replied:

I'll make sure they brush their teeth after they finish their Red Vines and Pepsi.

And jumping on the furniture?

They got bored with that already. Now we're in a fort made out of sofa cushions.

He immediately followed that up with another message:

Question—was the green marker stain always on the flowered chair cushion?

Her reply was quicker than he'd expected:

I'm going to assume you're joking because I'm off to track down more ice chips for my sister who's busy trying to have a baby while you're practicing your stand-up comedy routine.

Are you laughing?

She didn't respond, which he took to mean that she was either not amused or preoccupied with her search for ice.

So he settled the kids in front of the TV to watch an episode of their favorite (and mom-approved) program on Nick Jr. While they were engrossed in the animated adventures of rescue hero canines, he searched on his phone for current hockey scores and discovered there was a game on—he glanced at the clock on the wall— right now.

"Can we watch one more? Please, Uncle Mitch?" Elliott asked, when the episode ended with—surprise!— the Paw Patrol saving the day.

"P'ease?" Avenlea beseeched.

"Not tonight," he said. "It's already past your usual bedtime and the Golden Knights are playing the Dallas Stars."

"Can I watch the game with you?" Elliott asked.

"Past your bedtime," Mitch said again.

"But my bedtime is later than Avenlea's," the boy reminded him.

"You can stay up until the end of the second period," he relented, since it was just about to start.

Avenlea poked out her lower lip, clearly unhappy with what she saw as favored treatment of her brother.

"And you can pick two stories to read before lights out," he said, not above bribing her to turn that frown upside down.

It worked.

Avenlea skipped happily up the stairs to choose her books.

While she was sorting through the titles on her book-shelf, Lindsay texted again:

And don't let Avenlea con you into more than one story.

Too late.

* * *

Of course, it took the little girl almost as long to pick the books as it did for him to read them, but he finally closed the cover on *Lovabye Dragon*, pulled her covers up under her chin, kissed her forehead and wished her "sweet dreams."

He'd just settled back on the sofa with Elliott— eight minutes already gone in the first period—when the phone rang.

Though Lindsay had considered giving up the landline (with the same number he'd memorized when they were in grade school, before everyone and their brother had cell phones), she was reluctant to do so "in case of emergency." He considered letting the call go to voice mail, but he didn't want the ringing to disturb Avenlea, who was hopefully, finally, asleep.

"It's probably Gramma," Elliott told him. "She's the only one who calls that number."

"Gramma D or Gramma T?" Mitch asked. Not that it mattered—he was going to answer the phone regardless.

"T," the boy responded. "Gramma D calls on the computer."

He grabbed the phone on the third ring. "Hello?"

"I'd like to speak to Lindsay, please."

Elliott had guessed correctly—it was Gramma T.

Mitch probably would have recognized Suzanne Thomas's voice even without the boy's forewarning, but she obviously didn't recognize his. Or maybe she just didn't expect him to be answering Lindsay's phone.

"She isn't here right now, Mrs. Thomas, but I'd be happy to take a message," he said.

"Where is she?" Suzanne asked, sounding perplexed by the possibility that her daughter-in-law would be anywhere but at home with her children.

And while he wouldn't have freely given the information to anyone else, he figured it was a safe bet that Suzanne knew Lindsay's sister was near her due date. "She's at the hospital with Kristyne."

"Her sister's having her baby?"

"That's the plan."

"But…who's watching Elliott and Avenlea?"

"I am, Mrs. Thomas," he said, torn between amusement and exasperation. "That's why I'm here."

"But…surely you have better things to do on a Saturday night than babysit," Suzanne said. "Lindsay should have brought the children here."

"I think Lindsay was eager to get to the hospital and I happened to be in town," he said, not wanting Elliott and Avenlea's grandmother to feel slighted by the arrangements that had been made.

"Still, she should have called me and Arthur," Suzanne said. "After all, we're the grandparents."

"And I'm one of the godparents," he reminded her—the other one being Kristyne, who was otherwise occupied at present.

"I'm sorry. I didn't mean to imply that you aren't capable," she said. "I just worry that Lindsay relies on you too much, that she sometimes takes advantage of your affection for her—because she was married to your best friend."

"You don't need to worry about me," he assured her, not fooled for a minute by her fake apology or concern.

"Well, just let Lindsay know that I called," she said.

"I will," he promised, and went to watch the last five minutes of the second period.

Elliott went up to bed without further protest when the buzzer sounded, obviously tired out and ready to call it a day. In fact, he was drifting off before Mitch finished reading his chosen bedtime story.

But Avenlea woke up midway through the third period, asking for Mommy. Though Mitch wasn't sure Lindsay would approve, he took the little girl down to the family room to snuggle with him while he watched the end of the game.

Just when her eyes started growing heavy again, Elliott woke up and made his way back downstairs to ask if there was any news from the hospital. Realizing that his sister was awake, of course he insisted on staying up, too. And that's how Mitch ended up sandwiched between them on the sofa.

Lindsay was exhausted—both physically and emotionally—when she slid behind the wheel of her SUV to make her way home. But witnessing the miracle of her niece's birth had brought back so many memories, and she sat in the parking lot for a long while letting the tears stream down her face as memories flooded her heart.

It was the middle of the night when Lindsay had gone into labor before Elliott was born, so of course Nathan was there for that. Her contractions started almost immediately after her water broke, and so they put her overnight bag—already packed because she was a week overdue—into the SUV and headed to the hospital in Fairbanks. It turned out there was no reason to hurry—their son wasn't born until sixteen hours later.

Two and a half years after that, Avenlea decided to make her appearance in the middle of the day precisely on her due date—when her dad was at work and tied up in an important meeting. Thankfully they lived next door to a wonderful couple who had a son a few months older than Elliott, and Tammy offered to stay home with both the boys while Rita drove Lindsay to the hospital. Nathan had met her in the delivery room, arriving just in time to cut the umbilical cord.

She'd cried then, too. Overwhelmed by love for her daughter. Grateful and relieved that her husband had made it to the hospital in time to share at least part of the experience. And frustrated—and maybe even a little bit angry—that he'd come so close to missing the monumental event.

He'd promised her then that he would always be there for the important moments, and though she knew it wasn't a promise he ever wanted to break, he'd done so anyway. An undiagnosed mechanical issue with a plane flown by an inexperienced pilot had taken his life and so much more. So while Lindsay was overjoyed for Kristyne and Gabe, and excited about the beautiful new addition to their family, she was also all too aware that happiness could be fleeting and there were no guaranteed tomorrows.

Wiping the tears from her cheeks, she sent a quick message to Mitch to let him know she was on her way home. When he didn't reply, she guessed that he'd probably fallen asleep on the sofa, watching some game or another on TV.

Half an hour later, she toed off her shoes by the door and set her purse inside the coat closet, then quietly made her way to the family room. Sure enough, the TV was on, tuned to one of those all-sports channels that had likely shown a Golden Knights game earlier but was now recapping all the action from around the league that night. She expected that Mitch would be stretched out on the sofa, making use of the blanket and pillow she'd left for him. Instead, he was asleep sitting up, with her son tucked against one side and her daughter the other.

And the heart that had taken an emotional beating over the past several hours filled with so much joy it actually felt as if it was pressing against her ribs.

Because life was good, she realized.

And Mitchell was a good man who filled so much of the void that had been left after Nathan's death— a friend whose support meant the world to her. And even if the memory of his kiss was enough to make her knees weak and her body yearn, their friendship was too important to her to risk for the chance of something more.

She moved closer and carefully picked up Avenlea, trying not to disturb Mitchell. Of course, he immediately woke up when the weight of the sleeping child was lifted away from his side.

"You're home." His voice was rough and his eyes clouded with sleep.

"No, you're dreaming," she whispered teasingly.

"If I was dreaming, you'd be naked," he countered.

Warmth rushed to her cheeks, and a different kind of heat stirred in her belly.

"Sorry," he apologized gruffly. "My brain is still half-asleep."

"Luckily both Elliott and Avenlea are completely asleep," she said. And too young to understand, even if they'd happened to overhear his comment.

However, the implication of his teasing words was as clear to Lindsay as the awareness that suddenly sparked between them again. But with her sleeping daughter in her arms, this was neither the time nor the place to let her thoughts meander down that path.

She started to nudge Elliott awake, because he was getting too heavy for her to carry, but Mitchell halted her effort.

"I've got him," he said.

"Are you sure? I thought you were still half-asleep yourself."

"I'm awake now," he assured her.

So he carried Elliott up the stairs and tucked him into his bed, while she did the same with Avenlea. Of course, she checked on Elliott, too, because that was part of her usual nightly routine. She saw *Brady Brady and the Runaway Goalie* on the nightstand, and knew that Mitchell had read with him before he'd gone to sleep, understanding the importance of their nightly routines even when there was a hockey game on TV.

She'd wondered, more than once, how it was possible that he wasn't already married with half a dozen of his own kids running around the Circle G. Because it was obvious to Lindsay that he was meant to be a dad.

He'd be quite a catch as a husband, too, for whatever lucky woman managed to snag him. He was handsome, charming, sweet, sexy—and she hoped that someday he'd find someone who could appreciate all of his wonderful attributes and what a truly great guy he was.

As for herself, she needed to stand on her own two feet, to prove to him that she could. He'd done so much for her over the past two years that she'd become dependent on him, and that wasn't fair. Despite the fact that he'd always looked out for her, he wasn't responsible for her.

She wasn't a child anymore who needed a friend to walk her to the nurse's office for a Band-Aid when she fell down in the playground and skinned her knee. Or a naive teenager who didn't know what Jeremy Falconi had in mind when he invited her to eat lunch with him in the back seat of his new Mustang. And yeah, Mitch had saved her then, too.

Maybe she should have been embarrassed to be caught fending off Jeremy's grabby hands, but she'd been too grateful to Mitch for yanking open the car door and pulling her out of harm's way to feel any shame. Not until Nathan, coming upon the scene a split second later, had made fun of her innocence and naivete. In response to which Mitchell had told him to shut the hell up.

She knew that Nathan hadn't meant to be cruel, but his mockery had stung and Mitchell's defense had soothed. Much later, Nathan would acknowledge that he'd been a bit of an ass to her in high school because he'd liked her but hadn't wanted her to know it. He'd certainly succeeded in that regard. In fact, he'd done such a good job that she'd sometimes wondered how it was possible that she and Nathan, who could hardly stand one another, could both be friends with Mitchell.

And then, seemingly out of the blue, Nathan had asked her to go to the junior prom with him.

She'd been so shocked by the invitation, she'd actually stammered while trying to come up with a reply. In the end, she'd told him that she had to check with her mom before she gave him an answer, but the truth was, she'd wanted to check with Mitchell.

Because she hadn't really dated anyone before then. She'd occasionally gone out with a group of friends and sometimes one of the guys would express an interest in "going somewhere a little more private," but she'd declined all those invitations, feeling more comfortable in the crowd—where Mitchell was close by.

She'd been even more wary after the incident with Jeremy Falconi, and if she liked someone, she'd ask Mitchell's opinion, wanting to know if he was a good guy or if she should steer clear. He usually advised her to steer clear, claiming that even the good guys were "not good enough for you." Every single time, he came up with some reason that she shouldn't go out with a guy she was interested in.

Until Nathan.

Was it true that he'd only asked her to the prom because he'd known that Mitchell intended to ask her?

Whatever his reasons, she was glad she'd said yes to his invitation, because he'd been charming and sweet and she'd fallen just a little bit in love with him that first night. And even if she'd known then that their time together would be limited, she wouldn't change a minute of it, because without Nathan, she wouldn't have Elliott and Avenlea, and they were her everything.

Making her way back down the stairs again, she found Mitchell in the kitchen and the kettle just starting to boil.

"Since when are you a tea drinker?" she asked curiously.

"It's not for me, it's for you," he said. "I figured you'd be pretty wound up after all the excitement at the hospital and my mom swears that a cup of chamomile tea—which you conveniently had in your cupboard—helps her relax and sleep."

"You're always taking care of me," she remarked, as she dropped into a chair at the table.

"It's just a cup of tea," he said.

But it wasn't.

He'd done so much for her, and not just tonight, and she knew there was no way she could ever repay him.

"Boy or girl?" he finally asked, as he poured boiling water over the tea bag in her favorite mug.

She smiled. "Girl. Harper Rose. Eight pounds twelve ounces and twenty-two inches."

"Is that big?"

"Bigger than both of mine," she said. "Elliott weighed in at seven twelve and Avenlea was seven seven—with a bonus of three stitches for me."

He winced and quickly changed the subject. "Did Gabe make it back in time to see his daughter born?"

"He walked into the delivery room just as the doctor gave Kristyne the okay to start pushing."

"And then you got kicked out?" he guessed, setting the mug of hot tea in front of her.

"No." She smiled again. "They let me stay. And it was so amazing." She blinked away the moisture that filled her eyes. "And yes, I know I've been through childbirth before, but it was still an incredibly beautiful and emotional experience.

"So thank you," she said. "It was easy for me to focus on my sister tonight and not worry about Elliott and Avenlea, because they were with you."

"So texting to check in every ten minutes is what you do when you're not worried?" he teased.

"The texting was more to pass the time, because not much was happening in the beginning," she explained. "And I shared our messages with Kristyne, to distract her."

"From the pain of nothing happening?" he asked dryly.

"Even in the early stages, it's called labor for a reason." But Lindsay knew that her sister had been worried, too, about Gabe getting there on time. Or at all. And while she'd done her best to keep her mind off her husband's absence, she'd been as relieved as Kristyne when he finally arrived.

"Well, I appreciate your faith in me," Mitch said now. "Unfortunately, your mother in law doesn't share it."

"Suzanne called?" Lindsay guessed.

He nodded. "And wanted to come over when she found out that you'd left me in charge."

"She just wanted an excuse to come over and see the kids," she said, lifting her mug to blow on the hot tea.

"Maybe." He sounded doubtful, but moved on then to ask, "Did you get something to eat at the hospital?"

She shook her head. "No."

"Why not?"

"Because the hospital has a 'nothing by mouth' policy for women in labor, in case they need to be sedated, and I didn't want to eat in front of my sister."

"But you could have snuck down to the cafeteria for a snack."

"Is that a guy thing?" she asked. "Because that's exactly what Nathan did when I was in labor with Elliott. Although he didn't sneak—he outright told me that he was going to the cafeteria to get a sandwich, because he was hungry. *I* was the one in labor for sixteen hours, but *he* was hungry."

He opened the cookie jar on the counter and pulled out a handful of cookies, setting them on the table in front of her.

"You're not you when you're hungry," he said, borrowing a popular candy bar slogan.

She laughed as she broke off a piece of cookie and popped it into her mouth. "So how was your dinner?"

"I taught Elliott and Avenlea a new word when we were eating," he told her.

"Did you swear in front of my kids?"

"Of course not," he said indignantly. "Their new word is crudités, which we had with our chicken fingers."

"You mean raw veggies?"

"Yeah, but they're listed as crudités on the menu at The Home Station," he told her. "So when Elliott complained about having to eat carrot sticks and cucumber wheels, I explained that they were actually French hors d'oeuvres—and if he wanted *crème glacée* for dessert, he had to eat his crudités."

"Two questions," she said. "One—when were you at The Home Station?"

"Tonight, actually," he admitted. "That's where I was when you texted about Kristyne."

"You were on a *date*?" She stared at him, horrified. "Why didn't you tell me that you were on a date?"

"Because it wasn't as important as the fact that your sister was going to have her baby."

"I could have asked Mrs. Renaldi to come over to stay with Elliott and Avenlea."

"They like me better than Mrs. Renaldi," he said.

"They like you better than everyone," she agreed. "Even me sometimes."

"That's because I'm cool Uncamitch." He said it as one word, the way that Avenlea did. "And you're the parent who has to enforce rules and bath schedules and bedtimes."

"Isn't that the truth?" Then she shook her head. "But you're not going to distract me that easily."

"Is that what I was doing?"

"Tell me about her," Lindsay said, still baffled—and secretly pleased—by the realization that he'd ditched his date when she'd texted him.

"I don't know very much," he hedged. "We didn't make it too far past the basic introductions before you texted."

"You could start with her name," she suggested.

"Karli, with a *K* and an *i*," he said. "Who recently moved here from Colorado, with a *C* and an *o*."

She lifted her brows.

He shrugged. "That's how she introduced herself."

"Does Karli with a *K* dot the *i* with a heart?" she wondered aloud. Then, immediately apologized. "I'm sorry. That was snarky and unfair."

"It was," he agreed. "Especially considering that you're the one who's been pushing me to open myself up to the possibility of a relationship."

"You're right. I'm sorry," she said again. And if she'd had second thoughts about the decision when she'd learned that he actually was dating other women, well, it was too late to change her mind now.

Wasn't it?

"Anyway, you said two questions," he reminded her. "And that was only one."

"Right." But she was still trying to wrap her head around the fact that he'd run out on a date to babysit her kids. Which she sincerely appreciated but didn't imagine was going to increase his odds of getting another date.

"Second question," he prompted again.

"Did you let Elliott and Avenlea eat the last of my rocky road ice cream?" she asked.

"They had vanilla with caramel sauce and sprinkles. Lots of sprinkles."

The way he specified *they* made her eyes narrow. "Did *you* eat all of my rocky road ice cream?"

"There really wasn't much left," he said in his defense, offering another cookie to her.

She playfully snatched it out of his hand. "You owe me ice cream."

"And I'll buy you some—as soon as I get my baby-sitting money," he promised.

She smiled as she bit into the cookie, appreciating his sense of humor as much as his camaraderie.

And reminding herself again that friendship was enough.

Chapter Eleven

"I was glad—if a little surprised—that you called," Karli said, as The Home Station server delivered the meals for what was their second attempt at a first date. "The way you rushed out of here last week, I was sure I'd said or done something to scare you off."

"I told you why I had to go," Mitch reminded her.

"Yeah, but the friend-with-the-sister-in-labor story sounded like one of those fake emergencies to get out of a first date gone wrong."

"She had an eight-pound baby girl. They named her Harper Rose."

"So not a fake emergency," she acknowledged, slicing into her juicy roasted chicken breast on a bed of garlic mashed potatoes with a balsamic reduction. "Wait a minute—is your friend's sister married to Gabe Berkeley?"

"You know Gabe?" Mitch sampled his steak, unable to find fault with the chef's treatment of the Circle G T-bone.

"No, but I saw him play once, at a dive bar in Denver. The band mostly did cover songs, and not too badly, but it was obvious the drummer was the real talent. He nailed the solo in 'Hot for Teacher' so perfectly, Alex Van Halen would have been proud.

"Of course, most of his bandmates from back then are still jamming in dive bars while he's laying down tracks in the studio for chart-topping artists," she noted.

"I honestly didn't know he was that big of a deal," Mitch admitted. "He certainly doesn't flaunt his celebrity."

"He's that big of a deal," Karli assured him. "I follow him on Twitter, which is how I knew about the baby."

"What I want to know is why you thought our first date had gone wrong," he said.

"*I* didn't think it had, but some guys can't run fast enough when they find out I'm an engineer. It's one of the reasons I lead with that," she admitted. "I don't want to waste my time with a guy who's intimidated by smart women."

"Understandable," he said.

Karli studied him over the rim of her wineglass. "So tell me what you look for in a woman."

"I don't know if it's anything specific," he said, poking at an asparagus spear with his fork. "I've dated blondes, brunettes and redheads, women who were tall and short, skinny and curvy."

"So you don't have a physical type," she acknowledged. "But what about personality traits? What appeals to you?"

He shrugged. "I guess I like a woman who knows what she wants—and who's confident in who she is."

She nodded, encouraging him to continue.

"Someone who's loyal to her friends, good with kids and committed to family. Someone slow to anger and quick to laugh." An image of Lindsay laughing as she drank tea and nibbled on arrowroot cookies slipped into his mind, and he felt his lips curve.

"You're describing someone specific, aren't you?" Karli guessed. "I'm thinking...the single mom."

Busted.

"She fits the general description," he acknowledged.

"So why are you here with me?"

"I figured I owed you a meal—at the very least."

"You did," she agreed. "And while I appreciate that you're making an effort, it's obvious that you're not really into me."

He didn't bother to deny it. "I'm sorry."

"Don't be," she said. "I know it's you, not me."

He managed a wry smile. "Proving that you're every bit as smart as that fancy degree says you are."

She scooped up a forkful of mashed potatoes. "So how long have you been in love with her?"

He feigned ignorance. "Who?"

She rolled her eyes. "The single mom."

"We're just friends."

"Uh-huh," she said, clearly not buying it.

"I've known her since we were kids."

"In another word, forever," Karli mused. "So what's the problem? She doesn't feel the same way?"

"It's...complicated."

"It always is."

"She's a widow," he confided. "And her husband was one of my best friends."

"That is complicated," she agreed.

He nodded.

The conversation shifted to more generic topics as they finished their dinner and drinks, then Mitch paid the check and they walked out of the restaurant together.

"I'm sorry tonight was a bust," he said.

"It wasn't a complete bust," she said. "The meal was delicious—so thank you for that."

"It was the least I could do."

"You're right," she agreed. "And now I'm regretting my decision not to have dessert."

He chuckled. "Do you want to go back inside and order something to take home with you?"

She shook her head. "No, but thanks."

"I really did enjoy tonight," he told her.

"The night is still young." She kissed his cheek. "Go be with the one you want."

Lindsay glanced at the clock as she scrolled through the listings on her TV menu. It was nine o'clock on a Saturday night—the beginning of those long, empty hours between when her kids went to bed and she did.

Maybe she should get a pet. Elliott and Avenlea would love a dog or cat, and it would be good company for her. Heck, even watching a goldfish swim around in a bowl would be more interesting than anything on TV.

Or she could simply go to bed early. It had been a busy week, with all the excitement over Harper Rose and her parents' return to Haven to meet their newest granddaughter. But she didn't have Marilyn and Jackson for company, because they'd decided to stay with Kristyne and Gabe this time, to help the new parents with the baby.

Her cell phone chimed and she practically leaped to snatch it up off the table.

Are you up?

She replied:

It's 9 o'clock. What time do you think I go to bed?

As if she hadn't just been considering putting on her pajamas and crawling under the covers.

I try not to think about you in bed.

And though she knew she was treading on dangerous ground, she couldn't resist replying:

You try not to think about me in my bed? Or you try not to think about me when you're in bed?

Both are equally risky.

A statement of fact—and maybe also a warning.

I thought you had a date tonight. Why are you texting me?

I did have a date. And I'm texting because you haven't invited me to come in.

He was *here*?

She went to the windows and peeked through the blinds.

Yep, there was his truck in the driveway.

She hurried to the door and unbolted the lock.

"You're an idiot," she said, shaking her head as he stepped inside.

He grinned. "I've been called a lot worse."

"How long were you planning to sit in my driveway before letting me know that you were here?"

He shrugged. "Probably not much longer. Mrs. Renaldi pushed back her curtains at least three times, as if to let me know that she knew I was there."

"She *is* the unofficial neighborhood watch, you know." She moved back to the family room. "Do you want coffee?"

"No, thanks."

"So…how was your date?"

Considering that it was over before nine o'clock, she was surprised when he said, "Actually, it was great. It turns out that Karli's not just beautiful but smart and witty and fun. We shared a fabulous meal and interesting conversation."

She didn't particularly want to hear all the details, but she'd been the one to insist they remain firmly within the friend zone and, as a friend, it was her duty to listen.

"That is great," she said. *A lie.* "I'm happy for you." *Another lie.* "But I have to wonder, if she's so great… why are you here?"

"Because she's not you," he said simply. "And I don't want anyone but you."

She might have resisted the words, but the intensity and sincerity of his gaze sent them arrowing straight to her heart. Still, she had to be smart. To think about what was at stake.

"I know you're afraid to risk our friendship, and I understand why," he continued. "But there's so much more we could have together. So much more we could be to one another. Don't you think we deserve a chance to try?"

Before Lindsay could respond to either his confession or his question, he was kissing her. His mouth hot and hungry against hers, not asking but demanding a response. And she gave it, not just willingly but eagerly.

Her lips parted to allow him to deepen the kiss, and the sensual flick of his tongue against hers sent heat racing through her veins, making her burn. He kissed her until her mind was completely blank and her knees were weak.

Lucky for her, he had those strong shoulders that she could hold on to. He'd always been her anchor in the storm, but this time he was the cause of the chaos. He was responsible for the desire churning in her veins and clawing at her belly.

And then, just as suddenly as he'd taken her in his arms, he released her again, his breathing as ragged as her own.

"Just promise me that you'll think about it, okay?" he asked.

She nodded, certain it would be a long time before she'd be able to think about anything else.

On Wednesday, Mitch decided that an early-morning trip into town to pick up equine supplements from the feed store justified a quick detour to Sweet Caroline's. He ordered his coffee and, after careful consideration of all the options in the display case, a chocolate glazed—his tried and true favorite.

The popular bakery had limited indoor seating and when he looked around for a vacant chair, he spotted one at a nearby table where Heather was buckling her daughter into a high chair. She took a wipe out of her diaper bag and used it to clean the tray before she gave the little girl a sippy cup of juice.

Mitchell carried his coffee and doughnut over. "Do you mind if I join you?"

She looked around and seemed chagrined to discover there were no other empty seats available. "Of course not," she said, though her tone was less welcoming than her words.

"I forgot how busy this place can be in the mornings," he said, settling into the chair across from her.

"The Daily Grind is even busier."

"Better coffee there," he acknowledged. "Better doughnuts here."

"Do'," Silver said, stretching her arms to reach for the doughnut in front of her mother.

"Do you want a piece of doughnut?" Heather asked.

The little girl's wispy pigtails bobbed up and down as she nodded.

Mitch bit into his chocolate glazed.

Heather tore off a small piece of her cruller. "Say please."

"P'ease."

She set the doughnut on the tray and wiped her sugary fingers on a paper napkin.

"So where are you guys on your way to this morning?" he asked.

"From," Heather clarified. "We just came from story time at the library."

"Then you probably saw Lindsay. She works there part-time now."

Heather nodded. "I know."

Silver shoved the piece of doughnut into her mouth and reached her hands out to her mom again. "Mo'."

"Chew what's in your mouth first," Heather admonished.

Silver closed her mouth and chewed.

Heather smiled for her daughter, but the smile faded when she turned her attention back to him again. "What do you want, Mitchell?"

"I just thought it'd be nice to have some company while I drink my coffee," he said.

"Why don't I believe you?"

He shrugged. "There's no reason you shouldn't. *I've* never lied to you."

She didn't miss the emphasis. "Obviously you think someone else did."

"I could be wrong—" though his tone was conversational, he dropped his voice to ensure he wouldn't be overheard by anyone at the nearby tables "—but I'm guessing that Nathan at least twisted some truths to get you into bed three years ago."

Despite the color that stained Heather's cheeks, she met his gaze levelly. "There was no bed involved. We did it in the back of his dad's SUV—just like in high school."

Mitch wouldn't have broached the subject if he hadn't felt fairly confident that Nathan was Silver's father, but still, a part of him had hoped that Heather would shoot down his theory once and for all.

"But yes," she continued softly. "I think he twisted a lot of truths." She shifted her attention when Silver held out her open palm, offering a bite of doughnut to her mom this time, and the expression on her face morphed from guilt and regret to fierce and protective maternal love. "But I can't regret being played for a fool, because I ended up with Silver, and she's the best thing that ever happened to me."

She tore off another piece of doughnut for her daughter.

"But how did you know?" she asked Mitch. "She doesn't look like Nathan. Not really."

"But she does look like his son. And a little bit like his daughter. *Other* daughter," he clarified.

"You think so?"

He nodded.

She sighed.

"Did Nathan know?" he asked her now.

"No." She shook her head. "I was going to tell him I was pregnant. I thought he had a right to know—maybe even that he'd *want* to know. But then I found out that he'd gone back to his wife."

"You thought they separated?"

"Yeah. He always did know how to play me," she acknowledged ruefully. "But when he never reached out to me again, after we…reconnected, I suspected that the time we'd spent together hadn't meant anything more to him than an opportunity to relive high school."

Mitch couldn't defend his friend's actions—nor did he want to. In any event, while Heather might have been taken in by his lies as much as his charm, she clearly understood what Nathan was all about.

"Still, if you'd told him about Silver, he would have acknowledged her," he said, because he believed it was true. His friend might have been a bastard in a lot of ways, but he'd been a terrific dad who doted on his kids, and Mitch had no reason to believe the affection he felt for his children wouldn't extend to one born out of wedlock.

"My daughter deserved more than to be *acknowledged* as the bastard child of a cheating husband," she said tightly. "She deserved a father. A family."

"I guess it's lucky, then, that you were able to give her one."

"We *are* lucky," she agreed. "James is a wonderful husband and father."

"Does *he* know?"

"Of course he knows. I might have lied to my mother, because she couldn't keep a secret if it was handed to her in a locked box, but I wouldn't lie to my husband." She put the last piece of doughnut on the napkin in front of her daughter then looked at Mitch again. "Are you going to tell Lindsay?"

He scrubbed his hands over his face and swore under his breath. "I guess I'm going to have to," he said. "She needs to know."

"Does she, though?" Heather challenged. "I mean, what purpose would it serve?"

"At the very least, it would ensure she's not blindsided when the truth comes out—because the truth always comes out."

"No one has any reason to suspect that Silver isn't James's daughter," Heather said. "And anyway, he's been offered a big promotion at the company that would mean a move to El Paso."

"Do you really think moving out of state, away from your family, is going to keep your secret safe?"

"James and Silver are my family," she said. "And I'd go to the ends of the earth to protect them."

Mitch waited three days, but he wasn't sure he could wait any longer. He didn't want to tell Lindsay, but he really couldn't see any way around it. If she found out from someone else and then discovered that he knew but had kept the truth from her, she might never forgive him.

And it was inevitable that she would find out, because nothing remained a secret forever in Haven. Truthfully, he was a little surprised that people weren't already speculating about Silver's paternity. Although, the fact that Heather had given birth only five months after the wedding might have been enough of a scandal to appease the gossips—at least for a while.

But Mitch had no doubt that once the little girl was old enough to go to school—the same school that Elliott and Avenlea would be attending—the speculation would be fierce. Of course, Avenlea wasn't yet three, so she wouldn't be starting school for almost two years, and Silver would be a year after that. Or maybe Silver would be going to school in El Paso, if James Dekker decided to take the promotion that Heather had mentioned. So maybe there was no rush to tell Lindsay about her husband's infidelity.

Except that it was always risky to count on the truth remaining a secret. All it would take was one person to remark in passing that Heather Dekker's daughter had a smile just like Nathan Thomas's little girl, and the fact that Nathan had been in Haven nine months prior to Silver's birth would add fuel to the fire.

But before he said anything to Lindsay, he needed more information.

"Mitchell—this is a pleasant surprise," Suzanne Thomas said, greeting him with a smile.

"I apologize for dropping in uninvited," he said.

"Don't be silly." She stepped away from the door, a wordless invitation. "You know we're always happy to see you. In fact, Lindsay and the kids are coming over later for dinner, if you want to stay and eat with us. I've got a Circle G prime rib roast the oven."

He appreciated her loyalty to his family brand, but he had no appetite for dinner and even less for the conversation they needed to have. "Thanks, but I'll make this quick and get out of your way."

"Make what quick? Is there a problem?" she asked, sounding more curious than concerned.

He thought about the little girl with the sweet smile and big blue eyes—an innocent child caught up in a web of lies woven by the adults in her life, and he needed to know who was complicit. He didn't want to tarnish Suzanne and Arthur's memories of their son, but if Mitch's instincts were correct, he wouldn't be telling them anything they didn't already know—or at least suspect.

"I wouldn't say it's a problem so much as a situation," he replied to her question.

"Come into the kitchen," she suggested. "I've got potatoes on the stove."

He took off his boots and followed her across the mosaic ceramic tile floor, down the dark paneled hallway illuminated by crystal sconces. Like all the other houses on Miners' Pass, the Thomases' home was spacious and beautiful, though the decor was a little formal for his taste. It was difficult to imagine sticky fingerprints on the fridge or toys scattered across the Aubusson carpet in the front parlor—and seriously, who had a parlor these days?—but according to Lindsay, Elliott and Avenlea loved spending time at Gramma and Grampa T's. But perhaps Suzanne and Arthur had relaxed their previously strict house rules for their grandchildren, in the hope that they wouldn't someday run off to Alaska, as their only son had done.

Although Nate had been one of his best friends, Mitch hadn't been oblivious to the fact that he was selfish, spoiled and entitled. Not surprising, considering that he was an only child who'd always been given everything he wanted—or taken it, if it wasn't given.

But despite his flaws, Nate had loved Lindsay. If Mitch hadn't been certain of that, he never would have stood up for his friend at the wedding.

"Have a seat." Suzanne gestured to the trio of leather stools lined up at the island. "Can I get you something to drink? A beer, perhaps?"

"No, thank you," he said.

But he took a seat while she poked at the potatoes boiling in a pot on the stove.

"Is Mr. Thomas home?"

"He's in his office, reviewing briefs for a hearing on Monday—did you want me to get him?"

"No," he said, figuring she could fill in the details for her husband later—if he didn't already know. "There's no need to interrupt him."

She set down the fork and turned to face him again. "So what's on your mind?"

"Heather Dekker," he said, getting straight to the point.

Suzanne's perfectly shaped brows drew together. "I don't think I recognize that name," she said. "Should I?"

"She and Nate dated off and on in high school, when she was Heather Foss."

"He dated so many girls in high school." She shook her head a little. "It was hard to keep track of them all—until Lindsay."

Which was undoubtedly true, but her response was so deliberately vague that Mitch suspected she remembered more than she wanted to admit. Especially when he recalled a scene he'd witnessed outside of the funeral home at Nate's visitation.

He'd gotten caught up at the ranch and was late arriving, so he'd been surprised to pull in the parking lot and discover that his friend's mother wasn't inside accepting the condolences of family and friends, but outside with another woman, almost hidden from view behind an enormous stone planter. He'd only caught a glimpse of the other woman from the back as he turned into the drive, and by the time he'd parked and made his way to the entrance, she was gone and Suzanne was heading back inside.

He'd barely given it a second thought in the moment, more focused on being there for his friend's family than what he'd seen—which really wasn't anything at all. But after his conversation with Heather, he'd replayed the memory of that day and realized that the woman he'd seen Suzanne talking to might very well have been Heather.

Of course, *might* was hardly definitive. There were undoubtedly a number of women in Haven who were of a similar height and build with the same hair color as Heather, so maybe he should let it go. Whatever had happened between Nate and his ex-girlfriend, and whether Suzanne and Arthur knew, had nothing to do with him.

But it had a lot to do with Lindsay and Elliott and Avenlea. Nate's widow and children would inevitably be impacted when the truth came out. And that's why Mitch was here: for Lindsay.

"Did you know that Heather has a two-year-old daughter?" he asked now, watching Suzanne closely.

"No." She turned to pick up the fork and poke at the potatoes again. "And I'm not sure why you think that would be of any interest to me."

"Because her little girl has dark curls like Elliott and a smile just like Avenlea's."

"All children look alike to a certain extent," she remarked.

"She also has blue eyes like Nathan."

Suzanne stared at him, her expression darkening. "I don't like what you're implying," she said. "Maybe you should go now."

But Mitch wasn't going anywhere until he had the answers he came for.

"Silver is Nathan's daughter, Mrs. Thomas. Your granddaughter."

"That's a lie," she snapped, the polite facade gone. "I know my son wasn't perfect, but he's gone now, and I'd appreciate it if you didn't disparage his reputation."

"I'm not trying to disparage his reputation. I just want to know if you knew that he broke his wedding vows," he pressed.

"I don't believe that he did," she said, still firmly in denial.

Or maybe not so firmly, he mused, noting that she kept her gaze averted as she straightened a tea towel hanging on the oven door that didn't need straightening, and adjusted the angle of the knife block.

"But you suspected something," he realized.

Her hand trembled slightly as she repositioned the salt and pepper shakers.

"I know you think you're protecting Nathan's memory," he said. "But what about Lindsay? Have you given any thought to what it will mean to her?"

"If you were really concerned about Lindsay, you'd drop this right now," she said.

He'd told himself the very same thing, but he knew that secrets never remained secret forever. "She's going to find out," he said. "You know she is. I'm just trying to put the pieces together so that I can figure out a way to control the narrative and hopefully lessen her pain."

"Lindsay is the daughter I never had," Suzanne said, obviously wavering. "I couldn't love her any more if she was my own."

"Then tell me what you know, please."

She picked up the tea towel again, deciding to fold it now. "That woman stopped by, about six weeks after Nathan was home for my sixty-fifth birthday party," she finally said.

"Heather?" he asked, needing to be certain.

Suzanne nodded. "She wanted to know how she could get in touch with Nathan, because the number he'd given to her was no longer in service."

"Six weeks," he echoed. "So probably around the time she realized she was pregnant."

"I don't know," his friend's mother said again, her tone more weary than angry now. "She didn't tell me why she wanted to contact Nathan and I didn't ask. But I did tell her that whatever she thought she needed to talk to him about, it couldn't be important enough to bother him when he and his wife were celebrating the birth of their second child, and she agreed."

"And that was it?" he asked incredulously.

"She never came here again," Suzanne said. And in her mind, clearly that was the end of it.

But she'd shown up at the funeral home, Mitch was certain of that now. Of course, a lot of Nathan's friends from high school had been there to express their condolences—though Heather was the only one he'd seen having a tête-à-tête with Suzanne. "You're telling me that you never wondered—not even when, several months later, you must have heard that Heather was pregnant?"

She lifted her chin. "It wasn't any of my business. And she was married by then anyway."

"But you suspected that your son had cheated on his pregnant wife—and you didn't even ask him about it?"

Chapter Twelve

Before Suzanne could respond to his question, a shocked gasp sounded from the kitchen doorway.

Mitch's head swiveled to where Lindsay was standing, her expression stricken, a pie plate trembling in her grasp, and he silently cursed himself for being the cause of the pain he'd wanted only to spare her.

"You're early," Suzanne said to her daughter-in-law. "We weren't expecting you until four."

Lindsay's gaze shifted from her mother-in-law to Mitch and back again. "As soon as Grampa T told them the bunk beds had been delivered, they started pestering me to come over, but we had to wait for the pie to come out of the oven."

"Are they with Grampa now?" Suzanne wondered,

rescuing dessert from her daughter-in-law's tenuous grasp. "Did Arthur take them upstairs to see the beds?"

Lindsay nodded, then gave her head a slight shake. "Can we backtrack for just a minute here?"

"Sure," Suzanne said, sounding anything but certain.

"Is it true… Did Nathan…did he have an affair?"

Suzanne looked at Mitch—a wordless plea for help.

But he couldn't help her, not when the truth could only cause Lindsay more pain. He rose from his seat but resisted the urge to go to her, understanding that she needed time to accept the awful truth that she was hearing.

"Nathan loved you," Suzanne said. "You have to know that."

"I didn't ask if he loved me." Lindsay's voice quavered, just a little. "I asked if he had an affair."

Her mother-in-law's eyes filled with tears. "I don't know."

Lindsay turned to Mitch then. "Damn it, Mitchell. Tell me the truth. Did Nathan have an affair?"

She was obviously shocked and shaken, and well on her way to feeling the devastation he'd wanted to spare her. But he couldn't lie; he wouldn't be part of the deception. He nodded slowly.

"With Heather?"

He nodded again.

"And you knew." The anguish in her eyes and the raw tone of her voice gutted him.

She obviously felt betrayed, not just by her husband but by her friend, and he couldn't blame her.

"Why don't you sit down?" Suzanne suggested, the

tea towel now twisted in her hands. "Let me put on the kettle to make you a cup of tea and—"

"No!" Lindsay closed her eyes and exhaled a long, slow breath. "No, thank you."

"Please sit down," her mother-in-law urged.

Lindsay shook her head. "I can't. I have to go. I need to think."

Suzanne immediately protested. "But dinner's almost ready and the kids—"

"Ohmygod. Elliott and Avenlea." She pressed her hands to her cheeks, her eyes shiny with unshed tears. "Can they stay here for a while?"

"Of course they can," Suzanne said. "But you should stay, too. Give yourself some time to—"

"I can't," Lindsay said again, her voice raw. "I really just need to be alone right now."

And with that, she turned and fled.

Lindsay felt hot and trembly and sick to her stomach, and she prayed that she'd make it home before she threw up. Tears burned the backs of her eyes, but she refused to give in to the need to cry. Not yet. She wouldn't fall apart until she was alone—and then she was most definitely going to fall apart.

Relief rushed through her body when she pulled into her driveway. Almost immediately, Mitchell's truck parked behind her vehicle. She pretended she didn't see it as she made her way toward the front door, dropping her keys twice as she attempted to unlock it.

He gently took the keys from her hand to complete

the task, making it impossible for her to ignore him any longer.

"Thank you," she said stiffly. "But I really want to be alone right now."

"I don't think you do," he told her.

"Well, you don't always know what's best for me," she argued, blocking the now open doorway.

"Maybe not," he acknowledged. "But I know that you must have questions, and I might be able to fill in some of the blanks for you."

"That's right," she said, nodding. "Because you knew that my husband cheated and didn't tell me."

"I didn't know anything for certain until a few days ago."

"But you obviously suspected something before then," she noted, stepping away from the door to let him enter.

He followed her into the kitchen. "When I saw Heather at The Trading Post early in January," he admitted.

"What happened? Were you in the middle of the canned goods aisle and she just blurted out that she'd slept with my husband?"

"No." Mitch shook his head, cringing inside at the realization that Lindsay had only overheard the last part of his conversation with her mother-in-law, so she knew only part of the story. And not even the biggest part.

Which meant that he was going to have to be the one to tell her the rest. And in that moment, he actually hated his dead friend for what he'd done, leaving him to—if not clean up the mess—at least try to explain it.

He thought back to that day when he'd almost literally run into Heather and Silver and said, "It was the frozen food section."

Lindsay gave him an incredulous look. "Well, that makes a lot more sense."

"I didn't mean to say that out loud," he admitted, scrubbing his hands over his face. "I never wanted to be the one telling you any of this. Honestly, I wish there was nothing to tell."

"Yeah, I'm sure this is hard for you," she said, her voice fairly dripping with sarcasm.

"Can you please just listen to me for two minutes so that I can get this out?" he asked wearily.

She pressed her lips together.

"And maybe you should sit down," he suggested.

She remained where she was standing, facing him with her back to the counter, her fingers wrapped around the edge so tightly her knuckles were white. "Just tell me."

This was not at all how he'd imagined the truth coming out, but he had no one to blame but himself. As soon as Suzanne had said that Lindsay and the kids were going to be there for dinner, he should have given up on the idea of talking to her about Nathan's affair.

But hindsight was always 20/20.

"When I saw Heather, she was shopping for her daughter's second birthday. This was early January— just a week or so after the New Year.

"I knew she had a child," he continued. "I'd even seen her with Silver a couple times before, but I never knew—or realized—that she was born nine months after Nate was home for his mom's birthday."

"No." Lindsay's already pale face turned impossibly whiter.

He nodded grimly.

"It's not true," she said. "It can't be true."

"I'm so sorry, Linds."

She shook her head, refusing to believe what he was telling her. But the stricken look told him that she knew the truth, deep in her heart.

"No. There's no way…it's not possible." She pushed away from the counter and moved across the room. "Why are you doing this? Are you trying to hurt me?"

"No. Never." He started toward her, instinctively wanting to offer comfort. But he knew she wouldn't accept it from him. Not now when she blamed him for her world crashing down around her. So he stopped halfway and shoved his hands into his pockets. "Do you think this is easy for me? Do you think I *want* to be telling you this?"

She turned to face him then, and the sight of the tears on her cheeks was like a knife through his heart.

"You have to know I wouldn't be telling you this if I wasn't one hundred percent sure."

Lindsay did know, and that was why it hurt so much.

Because Mitchell would never lie to her about something like this. But he'd kept the truth from her, and that was almost as bad.

"I didn't want to believe it, either," he told her. "And at first, I tried to convince myself that the timing was nothing more than a coincidence. Then I saw Heather again, just last week at Sweet Caroline's, and she confirmed that Nathan is her daughter's father."

She had to swallow the lump that clogged her throat before she could ask, "How do you know she's not lying?"

"Because she has nothing to gain by lying—and a lot to lose," he said.

"So it happened when he came home for his mom's sixty-fifth birthday," she realized. "When I didn't come, because I was seven months pregnant."

"No one's blaming you," he said gently.

But he was wrong, because she blamed herself.

Because why would Nathan have cheated on her unless he was unhappy in their marriage? Or bored with their sex life?

She'd had a difficult pregnancy with Avenlea. More nausea and fatigue, and almost zero interest in making love with her husband. The doctor had assured her that everything she was feeling was perfectly normal, but Nathan was clearly unhappy about the lack of affection she was showing him. Because he felt neglected, never mind that she was exhausted from caring for a toddler all day—and growing another baby inside her belly. *His* baby!

When he'd talked to her about making the trip to Haven for his mother's milestone birthday, she'd been disappointed that she couldn't be there to celebrate the occasion—and secretly relieved that they would have a few days apart. Just a few days in which she didn't have to feel guilty about not wanting to be intimate or, worse, having to fake interest.

So she'd said goodbye to her husband and son—because even though she couldn't make the trip, she knew it would mean the world to Suzanne to have her grandson there—certain that the time and space would be good for each of them. And she'd actually missed Nathan while he was gone. And she'd believed him when he told her he'd missed her, too.

But the truth was, he'd been too busy hooking up with Heather Foss to spare a thought for the pregnant wife more than twenty-five hundred miles away.

And who had been taking care of Elliott while he'd been screwing his ex-girlfriend?

Suzanne, no doubt. She would have been so thrilled to spend some extra time with her firstborn grandchild that she probably didn't even ask where Nathan was going, never mind what—or who—he was doing.

"Silver...that's a beautiful and unique name."

"It's something of a family name...on her dad's side."

As snippets of that conversation echoed in her mind, Lindsay remembered being struck by the peculiar phrasing of the other woman's remark. Heather hadn't said the name was from her husband's family but from her daughter's father's family.

God, what a fool she'd been, not making the connection between "Silver" and "Sterling"—her mother-in-law's maiden name and, coincidentally, Elliott's middle name.

She shook her head. "So while I was in Moose Creek with Nathan's baby in my belly, he was making a baby with another woman, putting his—"

"Stop," Mitchell said. "Don't do this to yourself, Lindsay. Please."

She swiped at the tears that had spilled onto her cheeks. "I remember when Nathan and Elliott came home from that trip, how excited I was to see them. They'd only been gone five days, but I'd missed them like crazy. Nathan said that he missed me, too. And for the next few weeks after that, he was uncharacteristically attentive, as if to prove how much."

She gave a short laugh. "At least, that's what I thought at the time. Now I realize that his actions were likely motivated by guilt rather than affection."

Guilt because he'd had sex with another woman.

Unprotected sex, obviously, since the act had resulted in a child.

And then he'd come home and had sex with her.

The realization that he'd put her at risk—willfully or not—made her stomach churn again. She knew she was clean, because Dr. Tam had insisted on running a whole gamut of tests when she took Lindsay on as a new patient when she moved back to Haven, so she could at least be grateful for that.

"I'm sorry I didn't tell you as soon I knew," Mitch said. "But I didn't know how. And I didn't want to hurt you."

She nodded and wrapped her arms around her middle, as if that might somehow help her hold it together. But emotions battered at her like waves, and she started to crumble.

"Lindsay?"

She heard Mitchell's voice as if from far away as her knees buckled.

He caught her. Of course he did. Because he was

always there for her when she needed him—even when she didn't want to admit how much.

His arms came around her, drawing her close. And then she was sobbing against his chest, soaking his shirt with her tears as emotions raged inside her.

She felt hurt. And angry. Betrayed.

Cheated.

But Nathan hadn't just cheated on her—he'd cheated on his family.

"How could he do this to me?" she asked. "To his children?"

"I don't know, Linds."

She pulled back a little, to swipe her hands over her tear-streaked cheeks. "Maybe I would have grieved less for the husband I'd vowed to love and cherish *till death do us part* if I'd known that he'd already broken those vows."

"I don't think that's true," he said. "Regardless of the mistakes he made, you loved Nathan—and he loved you."

"How could he cheat on me if he loved me?"

"I don't know the answer to that question, either," he said. "The only person who does is Nathan."

"And I lashed out at you, because he isn't here for me to lash out at."

He shrugged those broad shoulders, clearly unconcerned. "You needed a target and I was here."

Because he was always here for her.

The one person she'd always been able to count on. Strong and steady, just like the heart she could feel beating beneath her cheek pressed against his shirt again.

His hand slid up and down her spine, comforting her as she might comfort Elliott or Avenlea. She snuggled closer to his warmth, his strength, breathing in the familiar scent of his soap, of Mitchell.

She felt a stirring in her blood and was suddenly cognizant that the mood had shifted.

Awareness crackled in the air.

Mitchell held himself perfectly still as she slid her hands up his chest, fascinated by the contrast of hard muscle beneath soft flannel. But she'd always known he was a man of contrasts—strong yet gentle, fierce but kind, passionate and controlled.

Desperate to feel some of that passion now, she lifted herself onto her toes and pressed her mouth to his.

There were rules to the game, Mitch reminded himself, as Lindsay settled her soft, sweet lips against his.

And one of those rules was not to take advantage of an obviously emotional and vulnerable woman—a rule that wasn't easy to remember when every part of her body was pressed against every part of his, causing his own to react in a predictable fashion.

Another rule was not to let himself be taken advantage of   not even by the woman he'd wanted for longer than he was willing to admit. If Lindsay ever decided that she really wanted to be with him, there was no way Mitch would be able to refuse her. Unfortunately, he understood that her actions right now weren't driven by desire for him so much as a desire to get even with Nate.

Devastated by the discovery that her husband had slept with another woman, she was seeking revenge in the arms of another man. And as much as Mitch wanted her, he didn't want to be any part of that twisted scenario.

He took hold of her wrists—capturing the hands that were roaming all over his body—and held them away. "Lindsay, stop."

She blinked at him, confused by his abrupt withdrawal. "What? Why?"

"Because this isn't really what you want," he said gently.

"What are you talking about? Of course it's what I want," she insisted. "And isn't it what you said you wanted—to give us a chance?"

"I *do* want to give us a chance," he assured her.

"Then why are you pushing me away?" she demanded, sounding not just frustrated but hurt.

As if he'd rejected her.

As if he ever could.

"Because what you're trying to do now isn't about us—it's about getting even with Nate."

She took a step back, her expression stricken.

"You don't want *me*," he said, though it pained him to admit it. "You want to be with someone who isn't Nate, because you just found out that he was with someone who wasn't you."

"Ohmygod…you're right." She lifted her hands to cover her face. "I'm a horrible friend. A terrible person."

"Stop it," he admonished gently. "You're not either

of those things. You're just trying to deal with a brutal emotional blow."

"You should be furious with me," she said.

"I'll curse you while I'm freezing my balls off in a cold shower at home," he promised.

She managed a smile. "You really are the best man I know."

He kissed her forehead. "And when you decide you really want me and not just revenge on your husband, you know where to find me."

Chapter Thirteen

She was likely making a mistake, Lindsay acknowledged as she walked up to the front door of the brick and glass building that housed Haven Mutual Insurance. Two and a half weeks had passed since she'd found out about Nathan's affair, since she'd learned that her husband had fathered a child with another woman.

During that time, she'd told the story more times than she wanted to—to her sister, who'd responded that Nathan was lucky he was already dead because she would happily have killed him for breaking her heart; to her parents, who'd tried to console her long distance while she'd tried not to completely fall apart again; and to Quinn, who'd told her—not unkindly—to stop mourning what was lost and move on with her life.

But Lindsay was still hurt and angry—and frustrated

that the only person who could answer her questions was dead. And then she realized that wasn't entirely true, that there was someone else who might be able to provide some of the information she needed. Whether she would cooperate was an entirely different matter, but she had to at least try to have the conversation.

Her sister attempted to talk Lindsay out of it. Kristyne was certain nothing good could come of a confrontation with Heather. But she'd still agreed to let Avenlea hang out with her for a few hours anyway, insisting that the little girl was a big help with her baby cousin. And Lindsay knew that she had to deal with her past before she could move on with her future.

She'd heard that Heather was again working as a receptionist at the insurance company, albeit only part-time, so she'd called first—and then apologized for dialing a wrong number when she recognized her voice on the other end of the line. Just like high school all over again.

Her heart was pounding against her ribs as she walked up the stone steps to the entrance. The sliding glass doors opened automatically, giving her no reason to pause. Lindsay stepped inside the spacious reception area with a wide curved work surface of frosted glass. The waiting room was arranged like a living room, with comfortable chairs and sofas around a frosted glass coffee table that offered an assortment of magazines for browsing. There were two clients waiting, both occupied with their phones, a sign of the times.

Heather glanced up, the ready smile on her face

freezing in place when she recognized Lindsay. But she had a role and she played her part. "Can I help you?"

Lindsay shoved her hands in the pockets of her jacket as she stepped closer, so the other woman wouldn't see that they were trembling. "I was hoping we could talk," she said.

"I'm working."

"I know. But maybe we could get together on your lunch hour? Or after work, if that's better for you?"

"I appreciate your willingness to accommodate my schedule, but I can't imagine what you think we have to talk about."

"Can't you?" Lindsay asked.

Heather held up a hand as she answered a call. After a brief exchange, she connected the caller to one of the agents, then shifted her attention to Lindsay again. "I've got the late lunch today. Two o'clock."

"Do you want to meet at Diggers'?" she asked, thinking only that the proximity of the restaurant just down the street made it a convenient location.

Heather gave a short laugh. "No. I brought a lunch from home. Why don't you pick something up and we'll meet at Prospect Park?"

"You want to eat outside in twenty degree weather?" she asked dubiously.

"Do you have a better idea?"

"How about my place?" she suggested.

The other woman seemed wary of the invitation. "Am I supposed to know where you live?"

"355 Winterberry Drive. The same house I grew up in."

Heather had been there several times when they

were in grade school together—for birthday parties and even the occasional sleepover—and a few times in high school, when they were on the yearbook committee together.

"I guess that would work," Heather finally agreed.

Lindsay nodded. "I'll see you around two, then."

This was definitely a mistake, Lindsay decided, as she stirred the soup heating in a pot on the stove.

Did she really expect that Heather was going to tell all just because Lindsay had invited her into her home?

Because she certainly had no intention of baring her soul to "the other woman" in order to get answers to the questions that plagued her thoughts.

Then the doorbell rang, and she realized that it was too late now to stop the events that she'd set in motion. She also realized that, until she opened the door and saw Heather standing there, she'd been more skeptical than optimistic that the other woman would actually show.

"I made soup," Lindsay said, as she ushered Heather into the kitchen. "Actually, I heated up soup, from a can. Garden vegetable."

"I'm good." Heather held up her reusable insulated lunch bag covered with bright pink poppies.

It wasn't really Heather's style—or not the style of the girl Lindsay had known years earlier—but she could imagine it was something her daughter had picked out. Though Lindsay didn't really spend any one-on-one time with the kids at story time, she'd noticed that Silver always wanted to sit on a pink pillow—and that the color was a popular choice for her wardrobe, too.

"Do you want coffee? Or tea?"

"No, thanks."

She stirred the soup simmering on the stove.

"So… I'm guessing that Mitchell told you," Heather said, keeping an eye on her as she unwrapped the cellophane from her sandwich.

Lindsay nodded.

"And you invited me here to tell me that I'm a tramp and a home wrecker and you hope I rot in hell?" the other woman guessed.

"No," she said. Though admittedly those same and other descriptions and sentiments had popped into her head at one time or another over the past two and a half weeks. But in her more rational moments, Lindsay had forced herself to acknowledge that Heather wasn't to blame for what had happened—or not entirely anyway. "I wanted to talk to you because I have questions that I'd really like to ask my husband, but since he's dead and buried, you're my next best hope for answers."

"So this is a lunchtime interrogation." She started to rewrap her sandwich. "No, thanks."

"I know you don't owe me anything," Lindsay said. "But I'd hoped—as a wife and a mom—you'd appreciate my need for some answers."

Heather still seemed wary, but she settled back into the chair. "What do you want me to tell you—that he tried to deflect my advances, but I persisted until he finally stopped saying no?"

"I don't want you to lie to me." Lindsay ladled some soup into a bowl, though her stomach was in such knots, she knew she wouldn't be able to eat it. "I just want to understand."

"Okay," Heather relented. "The truth is, Nathan told me that you'd split up."

And how ridiculous was it, after everything else she'd learned about her husband in recent weeks, that it hurt anew to hear those words come out of the other woman's mouth?

How was it possible that finding out that he'd lied about the status of their marriage in order to get into another woman's pants was almost as heart-wrenching as the discovery that he'd cheated on her?

Had he removed his wedding ring to perpetuate the illusion that their marriage was over?

She didn't ask.

Because apparently there *were* some things that she didn't want to know.

"And you believed him?" Lindsay challenged, wanting to shift some of the blame for her husband's actions.

"I had no reason not to," Heather said. "He'd come home with his son—"

"Also *my* son," Lindsay interjected.

The other woman nodded. "And I asked how you were doing, and he said he didn't really know...that you'd chosen to stay in Alaska to pack up your stuff, and as soon as he got back, you were taking Elliott and leaving."

"I didn't *choose* to stay in Alaska," Lindsay told her. "I wasn't allowed to fly because I was almost seven months pregnant."

"I didn't know," Heather said quietly. "And maybe I

didn't want to know. My second divorce had just been finalized and I was feeling alone and lonely and being with Nate reminded me of simpler times. Happier times. And maybe it was a boost to my self-confidence, too, that he could want me again, after dumping me in high school."

Lindsay swirled her spoon around in her soup for a minute before she finally asked, "Did you…want to get pregnant?"

"No." Heather shook her head. "The possibility never crossed my mind. I went on the pill in high school, so I wouldn't have to think twice about birth control. And I stayed on it right up until me and Leon—husband number two—decided to try to have a baby. Obviously that didn't happen for us and, after the divorce, I didn't imagine that I'd have any need for birth control.

"But I'm not sorry I got pregnant, because I wanted a baby. Not with another woman's husband," she acknowledged ruefully, "but I wanted a baby."

"She's a sweet girl," Lindsay said, because it was true. She might want to hate Nathan and Heather—and maybe she did—but their daughter was an innocent child.

"She's my world," Heather said simply, sincerely.

Lindsay decided to stop pretending she was eating the soup and pushed her bowl aside.

"For what it's worth… I know what it's like to be betrayed by someone you love," the other woman confided.

"Your husband cheated on you?"

Heather nodded. "The first one."

"How did you find out?"

"Explicit text messages on his phone. Of course, he said it was a mistake and promised it would never happen again. And then it happened again."

"Is that why you divorced?" Lindsay asked.

Heather nodded. "And now you're wondering what you would have done if you'd found out, while Nathan was still alive, that he'd been unfaithful," she guessed.

Actually, she'd been wondering that for the past two and a half weeks.

"I never thought that I'd be one of those women who would stay with a man who cheated." Of course, she'd also never thought Nathan was the type of man to cheat. "But when I think about what we had…and that leaving would have meant giving up our family… I'm not sure I would have been strong enough to do it."

"I didn't leave Trey because I was strong," Heather said. "I left because it was easy. Because when that trust was broken, there was nothing holding us together.

"It's different when you have a family," she continued. "A family is something worth fighting for. I mean, obviously everyone's situation is different and there are all kinds of reasons to make the decision to stay or go. I'm just saying you shouldn't judge yourself for whatever decision you might have made."

Maybe she was right. And in the end, it was all just speculation anyway, because Nathan was gone and there was nothing left to fight for.

"Well, this conversation has taken a turn I wasn't expecting," Lindsay confided.

"For what it's worth, I *am* sorry you were hurt," Heather said.

She only nodded.

The other woman glanced at the clock. "I need to head back to work."

"One more question," Lindsay said.

Heather paused, and visibly braced herself.

"Did you change story-time groups at the library so that you wouldn't have to see me there?"

"I thought it would avoid any potential awkwardness—for both of us."

"You should switch Silver back to the Wednesday session."

"Why?" Heather asked warily.

"Because Irene is a great supervisor, but I'm a better storyteller."

Lindsay often thought about writing down words of advice for her daughter in the future. Today's advice would be: if and when you marry, don't bake a cake for your mother-in-law's birthday during your first year of marriage, because it sets a precedent of expectation that will trap you for all the years that follow.

And that precedent was why she was carefully swirling buttercream icing on a triple layer red velvet cake.

As a new daughter-in-law wanting to prove herself in the first year that she and Nathan were married, she'd made an angel food cake with fluffy white frosting and confetti sprinkles for Suzanne's birthday. Her mother-in-law had loved the cake so much that she'd remarked—no less than three times—how it was so much more personal than anything picked out of a display case at the bakery. So for Arthur's birthday,

Lindsay got out her baking supplies again and made a chocolate cake with raspberry filling and chocolate ganache frosting.

Of course, she hadn't made birthday cakes for her in-laws during all the years that she and Nathan had lived in Moose Creek, because the logistics of shipping a cake twenty-five hundred miles were simply too daunting. (Because yes, she'd looked into it.) Instead, she'd shifted her focus to card making, sending birthday wishes with a personal touch and a first-class stamp.

Then Nathan died and she moved back to Haven with Elliott and Avenlea, only a few weeks before Arthur's birthday. Despite dealing with her own grief and sadness, she could see that her father-in-law was struggling with the loss of his only son. And though she didn't imagine he felt like celebrating at all, she made a cake in the hope that it might cheer him up a little. And then, a few months later, she'd made another cake for Suzanne's birthday, reestablishing the precedent.

Unfortunately, she wasn't finding the same pleasure she usually did in baking this time. Now that she knew about Nathan's affair, she couldn't help but associate his infidelity with Suzanne's birthday. And was it an affair? A fling? And did it matter? Whatever terminology was used, she didn't want to be reminded of it.

So she'd enlisted Elliott and Avenlea's help. They were both old enough now to follow simple instructions, and she was confident their involvement would make the task more fun. They'd been happy to measure and mix—and they loved the cracking eggs part, but when it was time for the cake to be sliced into layers and frosted, she decided that was a task better tackled by adult hands and set them up in the family room to watch TV.

And finally, it was done, which meant it was time to get the kids ready for a visit to Gramma and Grampa's.

Elliott was precisely where she'd left him—in front of the television, but the spot where Avenlea had been sitting was empty.

"Where's your sister?" she asked.

He didn't glance away from the screen as he shrugged. "Don't know."

Lindsay bit back a sigh, silently acknowledging that a five-year-old shouldn't be responsible for his little sister.

"Avenlea?"

She wasn't concerned about her daughter's whereabouts. Avenlea wasn't the type to venture outside on her own, and even if she'd been so inclined, both the front and back doors were wired so that they'd beep when they were opened. But Lindsay knew there was a whole lot of trouble she could get to inside the house.

"Avenlea?" she called out again.

"Up here, Mommy."

She started up the stairs, following the sound of her daughter's voice. "What are you doing?"

The answer to that question was evident even before Avenlea proudly said, "I p'ay dwess-up."

"I see that." Her little fashionista had decided to pair an ivory silk-and-lace nightgown with her own Minnie Mouse top and purple corduroy pants, adding a strand of fake pearls around her neck, Kate Spade sling backs on her feet and more makeup than a courtesan at Sheri's Ranch.

Avenlea shuffled forward, her child's-size-seven feet struggling to master the art of walking in adult-size-eight shoes with a two-inch heel. Lindsay quickly scooped her up—rescuing her from the shoes before she tipped over and broke something more valuable than the heels.

"What you were supposed to be doing, though, was watching *Paw Patrol* with Elliott," she reminded her daughter.

Of course, it was her own fault for leaving the little girl unsupervised while she'd decorated the birthday cake. Yes, Avenlea had been given strict instructions to sit with her brother, but Lindsay should have known better than to expect she'd actually do so. Or to imagine that Elliott wouldn't be so engrossed in the program that he might actually notice if his sister slipped away.

But seriously, it had been no more than ten minutes. Fifteen at the most.

How could one little girl manage to do so much damage in such a short period of time?

It wasn't just the clothes spilling out of her dresser drawers or the contents of her jewelry box dumped out on her bed—it was also her makeup. Though Lindsay didn't often bother with more than foundation and mascara, she had some quality stuff for the rare occasions it was warranted. And she was pretty sure that was her favorite Estée Lauder "Potent" lipstick on the floor.

The fancy palette of eyeshadows—boasting thirty-two designer shades—had been a gift from Nathan one year for Christmas. And maybe she was ungrateful, but she felt that a gift of makeup from a husband was similar to that of a blender or a vacuum cleaner. But she'd occasionally lifted the heavy mirrored top and swiped a little "fawn" or "bronze" on her eyelids, so that she could tell him she used it.

It looked as though Avenlea had tried each and every one of the thirty-two shades, with a focus on the brightest colors in the palette. And she'd smeared blue and green and purple not just on her eyelids but all over her face.

"I wook pwe-ty?" she asked hopefully.

Like a rainbow fish, she thought, but knew her daughter would take that as a compliment.

"You look like you've got a lot of stuff all over your face," Lindsay said. "But I know my pretty girl is under there somewhere, so let's wash that stuff off and find her."

Avenlea folded her arms over her chest and shook her head. "No wash," she said stubbornly.

"Yes, wash," Lindsay insisted. "Because if we don't clean the makeup off, you might end up with itchy, bumpy spots."

The prospect of a rash motivated Avenlea to follow her mom into the en suite bath. Lindsay sat her on the counter and opened a blue jar. She applied the NIVEA cream carefully to her daughter's face, then dampened a soft washcloth with warm water to clean it off again.

"How did you even know how to put makeup on?" she asked, as she wiped gently with the cloth.

Avenlea scrunched her face up to protest the rubbing. "Gwamma."

"I can't imagine your gramma has ever worn blue or green or pink eyeshadow—and I guarantee you, she never wore all three colors at the same time."

"Pwe-ty co-wuhs."

Lindsay kissed the tip of her daughter's nose. "Pretty girl."

Avenlea beamed happily and lifted a hand to swipe at a hair that was stuck to her damp cheek.

That's when Lindsay saw what her daughter was wearing on her finger.

It seemed to be the story of his life—or at least the last two and a half years—that Mitch was making up excuses to drive into town and stop by the house on Winterberry Drive. At first, his visits had been motivated by concern for his friend, grieving the loss of her husband and struggling to adapt to her new reality as a single mom of two children. Children who were undoubtedly confused about the sudden changes in their lives and missing their dad. More recently, though, he'd been stopping by because he enjoyed hanging out with Lindsay and Elliott and Avenlea.

Spending family time with another man's family, according to his sister.

Luckily, he had a lot of experience ignoring his sister.

Today's excuse for stopping by?

"I owed you ice cream," he said, when Lindsay opened the door.

Her lips curved as she accepted the pint of rocky road. "And I still owe you babysitting money."

He waved it off, noting that her smile seemed a little strained at the edges. And when he looked at her more closely, he saw that her eyes were red-rimmed and her cheeks a little blotchy. "Have you been crying?"

"Apparently I don't wear enough makeup," she muttered, making her way to the kitchen to put the ice cream in the freezer.

"Huh?"

"Never mind."

The house was uncharacteristically quiet. "Are the kids in bed already?"

She nodded. "We had a busy day, and they both crashed early."

Which meant that the adults could chat without being interrupted—at least until Avenlea woke up, as he knew she did a couple of times each night, and wanted Mommy. So he took Lindsay's hand, led her into the family room and tugged her down onto the sofa beside him.

"Now tell me why you were crying," he said.

"You'll think I'm silly," she warned.

"Probably," he agreed, earning a small smile. "But tell me anyway."

"Avenlea decided to play dress-up today and got into my jewelry box…and she lost something that meant a lot to me."

"Not your wedding rings?" He'd noticed that she'd taken them off a few weeks earlier, after she'd found out about Nathan's infidelity, but of course she'd still be distressed if they went missing.

But Lindsay shook her head. "No. This was something I'd had a lot longer than those."

"The locket from your grandmother?" he guessed.

"No. And seriously, if I tell you, you're going to laugh because the only real value of the item is sentimental."

"It's okay," he said. "I already know you're a softy."

"It was my purple flower ring."

"You say that as if I should know what you're talking about, but I don't...wait a minute—do you mean the plastic ring that *I* gave you when we were kids?"

She nodded.

"I didn't realize you still had it." He was stunned—and absurdly touched—by this revelation.

He'd gotten the ring out of a vending machine at Jo's Pizza. He'd slid his quarter into the slot and hoped for a super bouncy ball as he cranked the knob to dispense his prize. When he opened the plastic clamshell container and saw the ring, he'd been deeply disappointed.

"What the heck am I supposed to do with a stupid ring?" his ten-year-old self had grumbled to his brother.

"Give it to your girlfriend," twelve-year-old MG had sneeringly replied.

"Lindsay?"

"You got another girlfriend?"

"She's just a friend," he said, because the word girlfriend *made him squirm ever since Megan Carmichael said she wanted to be his girlfriend and tried to kiss*

him by the monkey bars at recess. Thankfully, Mitch could run faster than she could.

But the thought of kissing Lindsay didn't seem nearly as gross.

"You think she'd want it?" he asked, looking at the ring again.

MG shrugged. "If you wanna marry her someday, you hafta give her a ring."

Mitch was only ten—he wasn't ready to think about getting married.

But he supposed that everyone had to get married eventually, so why shouldn't he marry Lindsay?

Still, he'd carried that ring in his pocket for four days before he got up the nerve to ask her—and she'd said yes!

And then he'd mostly forgotten about it...

"Well, I did still have it," Lindsay confided now, sniffling a little. "And now I don't."

"It'll turn up somewhere," he said confidently. "Like those Mr. Potato Head accessories you find stuck between the cushions in the sofa. Or the little LEGO bricks that you never see until you step on them."

"She was wearing it when we left to go see Gramma T for her birthday today, but it wasn't until I asked her to put it back in my jewelry box before she had her bath that we realized it was gone."

He slid an arm across her shoulders and hugged her close. "I'd get you another one if I could, but I'm pretty sure they've updated the prizes in those vending machines at least once or twice in the past twenty years."

"I don't want another one. I want the one you gave me."

She swiped at a tear that spilled onto her cheek while Mitch tried to think of something he might say or do to make her feel better.

"You do realize it was a twenty-five-cent ring, don't you?" he asked gently.

"Of course I do, but..."

"But what?" he prompted.

"You know how a bride is supposed to have something old, something new, something borrowed and something blue?"

"It sounds vaguely familiar," he agreed.

"Well, that ring was my something old, when I married Nathan."

"You had that plastic ring when you walked down the aisle?"

"It wasn't on my finger, obviously. But it was stitched to the bottom hem, on the inside of my dress. It was my first engagement ring, from the first boy who ever loved me."

And wasn't that an unexpected revelation?

Equally unexpected was the emotion that filled his heart, even if he wasn't able—or maybe not willing—to label it.

"Well, don't give up hope," he said. "I'm sure it will reappear somewhere."

Because now that he knew how much that ring meant to her, he would turn the whole town upside down, if he had to, to get it back for her.

Chapter Fourteen

Lindsay settled deeper into the leather, almost moaning with pleasure as whatever magical contraption was inside the back of the chair moved up and down and across, massaging her tight muscles.

"It feels good, doesn't it?" Quinn asked, relaxing in a matching chair beside her friend.

"Sooo good," she agreed.

"Now aren't you glad you let me talk you into this?"

"Sooo glad."

Quinn laughed softly. "Obviously you were overdue for some pampering."

"It feels so indulgent to sip wine in the middle of the afternoon," she said, as she looked over the rim of her wineglass at her "Crimson" painted toenails.

"That's the point."

"It's just hard to find the time when the kids are so busy. Elliott has school and even though hockey's over for the season, soccer will be starting soon, and Avenlea has story time and swimming and Tiny Tumblers."

"Your fault," Quinn responded without sympathy. "No one told you to schedule every minute of their every day."

"It's hardly every minute of every day."

"Then you should be able to squeeze out a few minutes for this every now and again," her friend said, cleverly boxing Lindsay in with her own words.

But they'd been at the spa for more than a few minutes—most of the afternoon, in fact. And she really wasn't feeling guilty at all that her daughter was spending the day with Suzanne, who was also going to pick Elliott up from school so that Lindsay didn't have to worry about keeping track of time, and then both the kids were going to spend the night at their grandparents' house.

Since the day Lindsay had overheard Mitch and Suzanne talking about Nathan's affair, her mother-in-law couldn't do enough for her—almost as if she was trying to make up for raising a son who could disregard his wedding vows. Not that she and Suzanne had actually talked about what they'd each learned that day, but the truth seemed to be a constant undercurrent in every conversation. And when Lindsay had finally given in to her friend's nagging and asked Suzanne if she could watch Avenlea for half a day so that she could enjoy some time at the spa with Quinn, Suzanne had encouraged her to take the whole day, insisting that she deserved it.

Which was why, by four o'clock in the afternoon,

she'd had a facial, a scalp massage, a manicure—with hot paraffin wax treatment—and a pedicure, and now she and Quinn were relaxing in the massage chairs, sipping wine and waiting for their nail polish to dry.

"This chair is great," Lindsay said now. "But next time, I'm going for a real full body massage."

"It's a good way to release the tension," Quinn said. "Not as good as hot, sweaty sex, but a decent alternative."

Lindsay sighed. "I can't remember the last time I had hot, sweaty sex. Truthfully, that might be why I want a massage—just to have someone touch my body."

"I know your coffee dates with Parker turned out to be a dead end, but I bet your hunky rancher would oil you up if you just said the word."

"He's not *my* hunky rancher," she denied.

"Only because you haven't admitted how much you want him," Quinn insisted, wiggling her "Mauve On Over" toenails.

"I want us to stay friends."

"Haven't you ever heard of friends with benefits?"

"It was a good movie," Lindsay said. "But the ending actually contradicts the title."

"And that's what you're afraid of, isn't it?" her friend guessed. "Falling in love."

"I'm not afraid of falling in love. I'm afraid of losing my best friend."

"You and Nate were friends first, too," Quinn reminded her. "And that worked out."

"If being widowed after five years of marriage, including at least one confirmed indiscretion, counts as working out," she remarked dryly.

"I wasn't thinking about that," Quinn admitted. "Only about how much you loved one another."

"Which actually proves my point," Lindsay said. "I've already lost Nathan. I don't know what I'd do if I lost Mitchell, too."

"If you don't snap him up, some other woman is going to," Quinn warned. "Then you really will lose him, because no wife in her right mind is going to accept her husband being friends with an attractive widow with whom he has a history."

"A history of *friendship*," she pointed out.

"Dotted with a few steamy kisses."

"Still, a few kisses isn't any reason for a future wife to disapprove of our friendship."

"And she might pretend to be okay with it at first, but it won't take long for her to come up with ways to keep him busy, so that he doesn't have time to hang out with you. But those ploys will only be necessary until they have a child, then he will be too busy with his family to trek into town from the Circle G to check on his old pal."

Lindsay swallowed her last mouthful of wine. "Well, good," she said. "He deserves to fall in love, get married and have a family. And anyway, you seem to be forgetting the part where I tried to seduce him and he wasn't interested."

"I've seen the way he looks at you, and I guarantee he wasn't not interested," Quinn said. "You just picked the wrong time to let him know that you wanted to get naked with him."

"You mean an hour after finding out that your husband cheated isn't the right time?" she asked dryly.

"No man with an ounce of self-respect would have done anything different," her friend said. "It doesn't mean he doesn't want you."

Which was pretty much what he'd said, when she'd apologized for her impulsive and pathetic attempted seduction.

"Go to him now," Quinn urged.

"It's Friday."

"Do you have some moral objection to sex on Fridays?"

"I haven't had sex in more than two and a half years. I think I'm good to go on any day that ends in a *Y*," Lindsay replied. "My concern is that Mitchell might actually have other plans."

"So call him," her friend said, with a wink. "And tell him it's his lucky day."

She wanted to talk.

As if they didn't talk—or at least exchange text messages—almost every single day.

And she didn't want to talk on the phone; she wanted to come out to the ranch, but only after ensuring that his brother wasn't home.

So while Mitch waited for Lindsay to arrive, he busied himself tidying up. Not that the place was untidy (because Angela Gilmore hadn't raised her kids to be lazy or messy), but he needed to keep busy so that he didn't make himself crazy wondering what she wanted to talk about that necessitated a trip out to the Circle G on a Friday night.

He was wiping down the mirror in his bathroom—he and MG each had their own—when a tentative knock sounded.

He opened the door to find Lindsay standing on the wooden porch, a long coat open over a dark green wrap-style dress with a scoop neckline and short skirt. On her feet were knee-high black boots with a sexy two-inch heel.

"Hi," he said.

"Hi," she said back, and then, "I found you."

"You texted to make sure I was home," he reminded her.

She nodded. "I meant… You told me that I'd know where to find you…when I figured out what I wanted."

Now he knew what she was talking about.

And she was at his door—*hallelujah*.

Still, he curled his fingers into his palms so that he didn't reach out and haul her into his arms until he was sure that she was sure. "Have you figured it out now?"

She nodded. "I want you, Mitchell."

There was no hesitation in her words, no flicker in her gaze. She was sure—and so was he.

He hauled her into his arms, dragged her over the threshold, closed and locked the door and kissed her until they were both breathless.

"Just to clarify," he said, when he'd drawn enough air into his lungs to speak, "you didn't actually come here to talk?"

"I didn't come here to talk," she confirmed. "I just didn't want to admit this was a booty call in my text message."

"Is that what you think this is?"

"I came here to have sex with you, so…yes?"

"Maybe, just for tonight, you could let go of your need to put labels on everything," he suggested as he slid his hands up her back, then down again. And realized that she was still wearing her coat.

"And let's get rid of this, too," he said, helping her remove the outer garment and tossing it over the arm of the sofa. Though he was a little reluctant to see them go, her boots followed.

"We're both still wearing too many clothes," she told him.

It was pretty much an invitation to strip her naked and take her right there, and he was admittedly tempted. But he'd wanted her for so long—and denied his own desires for almost as long—and now that she was here, now that the moment he'd been waiting for was finally at hand, he didn't want to rush it. He wanted to savor every second, every kiss, every touch. He wanted to love her like she'd never been loved before, so she'd remember this night—and him—forever.

But before they got too far, he had to know: "Where are Elliott and Avenlea?"

"It's sweet that you'd ask about my children at a time like this," she said. "But I kind of hoped we'd focus on you and me tonight."

"I'm focused," he promised, lazily exploring her curves with his hands.

"They're spending the night at Gramma and Grampa T's."

"Are you spending the night here?"

"I could…if you decide that you want me to."

"I want you to," he said.

"I meant for you to decide…after."

"Do you think I'm going to change my mind… after?" he teased.

"I've only ever been with one man," she confided. "You might be disappointed."

"I'm not going to be disappointed," he said, his tone serious now. "And I promise to do my best to ensure you're not disappointed, either."

"Okay." She exhaled audibly, then smiled as she reached for the tie at the side of her dress.

"Let me," he suggested, capturing her hand and drawing it away.

"I was letting you, but you were taking too long."

"Didn't we just establish that we have all night?"

"Yeah, but I was kind of hoping we might do it more than once in that span of time."

"And we will," he promised. "Just relax."

"More than two years," she reminded him. "How am I supposed to relax when I'm so tightly wound up, I feel as if I'm going to explode?"

And he was definitely looking forward to *that*, but first he asked, "Do you trust me?"

"There's no one I trust more," she assured him.

"Then trust that I'm going to take care of you," he said, leading her to his bedroom.

He closed and locked that door, too. Though he wasn't expecting his brother to return tonight, several other family members also had keys to the bunkhouse, and he didn't trust all of them to respect the boundary of the locked exterior door.

Now he reached for the tie of her dress and tugged to release it—only to discover another tie on the inside. But he made quick work of that one, too, and finally parted the fabric to reveal lots of silky skin and a pale pink bra and panty set.

His hands trembled as they skimmed over her body, eager to touch. He wanted to be gentle, but his palms were hard and callused—an inevitable by-product of the manual labor he did every day. It occurred to him that he should apologize for their roughness, but when she sighed, it was a sound of pure pleasure that assured him she didn't mind.

He took his time exploring every dip and curve, gauging her enjoyment by the soft sounds she made.

"And you wanted to rush through this part," he teased.

"I didn't know about this part," she said, as his lips trailed kisses down her throat.

"Now you know." He whispered the words against her lips—a prelude to another long, slow kiss.

"You're so good at that," she murmured.

"Kissing is like dancing," he told her. "It's all about your partner."

"That's kind of cheesy…and really sweet."

He knew she was worried that making love would change things between them, but everything had already changed. Starting at New Year's Eve with that first kiss, the feelings that he'd kept buried deep for so long had risen to the surface again, demanding to be acknowledged, urging him to take hold with both hands of the chance he'd been waiting for—the woman he'd always wanted.

His mouth skimmed along the lacy edge of her bra; she shivered.

"Are you cold?"

She shook her head.

Her nipples were already peaked. He could see the tips pressing against the delicate lace. He brushed his lips over one tight point, through the thin fabric barrier, and heard her breath catch. He swirled his tongue around the nipple, then over it. She arched her back, wordlessly seeking more.

He unsnapped the clasp between her breasts and gently peeled back the cups, baring her breasts to his hungry gaze and hungrier mouth. She gasped when his lips closed over the bare flesh, and moaned when he began to suckle.

"Mitch...oh..."

He slid a hand between her thighs, dipping a finger beneath the swatch of lace, and found her not just wet but dripping.

Now *he* groaned.

He hooked his fingers in the sides of her panties and drew them over her hips and down her legs. Then he held up a hand, wordlessly asking for silence. "I just need a minute to worship quietly."

The comment surprised a laugh out of her, but he hadn't been joking. Never had he been with a woman who was more perfect to him. Not in a lingerie model sort of way, but in a real woman way, with actual hips and narrow silvery lines on her abdomen—evidence of the babies she'd carried, the lives she'd borne.

"I know I'm not the first woman you've ever seen naked," she said.

"No," he admitted. "But this is the first time I'm seeing *you* naked."

"When do I get to see you naked?" she wanted to know.

"When I'm not worried about losing what little self-control I'm clinging to," he told her.

"Self-control is overrated," Lindsay said, reaching for his belt.

He let her have her way, cooperating with her efforts to rid him of his clothes. Shirt, jeans and socks were quickly tossed aside, but then Mitchell took the reins again.

His lips feathered lightly over her skin, caressing more than kissing, skimming the hollow between her breasts, her belly button and lower. He parted her thighs and settled between them, his unshaven jaw rasping against her tender skin.

She cried out his name as her release came, hard and fast. Her fingers curled in the sheet, grasping for purchase as wave after wave of sensation crashed over her, but he didn't let up.

It was almost more than she could stand, and yet, it wasn't enough. She wanted the fulfillment that she knew would only come when he was buried deep inside her.

"Mitchell…please."

He reached into the drawer of his bedside table then

and found a square packet, tearing it open and sheathing himself to ensure their mutual protection. Then, finally, he lowered himself into position and slowly eased into her, inch by inch, giving her body time to accept and accommodate all of him.

Her breath shuddered out of her lungs as he filled her.

"Okay?" he asked.

She nodded.

He started to move, slowly at first, and new waves of sensation began to build, churning like the sea before a storm.

Then faster. Deeper. Harder.

The storm was all around her now, battering at her from all directions. She held on to him, her hands clutching at his shoulders, clinging to her rock.

"I've got you," he promised, just before he captured her mouth again.

They were connected, from head to toe and in between. Two bodies joined in pursuit of one goal— mutual pleasure…and finding it together.

She was cradled in strong arms, wrapped in the warmth of his hard body. She didn't have the energy to move. Or maybe it was the will that she lacked. Yeah, it had taken them a long time to get here, but right now, she was exactly where she wanted to be.

Who knew that Mitchell would prove to be such an attentive and thorough lover? Well, any one of the women who'd found her way to his bed before Lindsay, but she wasn't going to think of them now. She wasn't going to think about anything but the fact that she was up close and personal with a naked man whose hard body was already showing a willingness to go another round.

"Quinn was right," she murmured, as he nuzzled her throat.

"About what?"

"She said that hot, sweaty sex is the best way to release tension."

"You were very tense," he noted.

She laughed softly.

And that was another surprise.

She'd been worried that making love with Mitchell would somehow change their whole relationship, because sex had a way of pulling back the curtain and exposing all of one's intimate secrets. She hadn't considered that Mitchell already knew her more intimately than anyone else ever had—that the only part of herself she hadn't shared was her body. And after even that had been given to him, she actually felt closer and more connected.

And when he rolled her onto her back and rose over her, they connected again.

Chapter Fifteen

Lindsay was happy when the spring sunshine finally melted the last lingering vestiges of snow from the ground. Or maybe it was her spring romance that was responsible for the lightness in her heart.

She enjoyed all the seasons, but the twice-daily journey to and from Ridgeview Elementary School was a lot easier when she didn't have to push Avenlea's stroller through snow and slush. Today her daughter had insisted on walking, and she wasn't yet sure if that was a bonus or not.

As they made their way along the familiar route, Lindsay found herself pausing in front of a two-story red brick house with white shutters. It had been Abe and Ethel Nicholson's house for as long as she could remember, then Abe died and Ethel moved to Elko to be closer to her son and grandchildren. The house had sold quickly and, according to the sign on the lawn, was for sale now again. But it was the woman cleaning the windows, side by side with a little girl, who caught her attention.

As if sensing her presence—or maybe she could see the sidewalk reflected in the glass—Heather turned around.

"Hey," Lindsay said awkwardly. "I didn't know you lived here."

"For now," the other woman agreed.

"Sto-wee!" Silver shouted, obviously recognizing Lindsay as a storyteller from the library.

"Hello, Silver." She urged Avenlea forward, to introduce the two girls. "This is my daughter, Avenlea. Avenlea, this is Silver."

"Hi," Avenlea said.

Silver responded with a shy smile and a wave.

Lindsay found herself looking from one girl to the other, searching for signs that they shared a father. She wasn't sure if she was relieved or disappointed that there were no glaring similarities, but there were definite hints of the little girl's paternity: the curls in her baby-soft hair were reminiscent of Elliott's curls; the cupid's-bow mouth was shaped just like Avenlea's; and the clear blue color of her eyes was Nathan's.

"I guess your husband decided to take that job in El Paso," Lindsay said.

Heather nodded. "He's there now, house-hunting."

"Are you looking forward to the move?"

"Change is always hard, but yes, I think it will be

good for all of us—and undoubtedly a relief to certain other people in this town."

Lindsay frowned, wondering who she could be talking about. Only a handful of people knew the truth about Silver's paternity and she couldn't imagine anyone—

"We crossed paths with Nathan's mom at The Paper Dragon," Heather told her, naming the specialty card and gift shop on Main Street. "Or maybe I should say we *almost* crossed paths with Nathan's mom, because when she saw us, she quickly turned the other way."

"I think she's uncomfortable acknowledging that her son had two daughters with two different women only eight months apart."

"Especially when one of those women was his wife."

Lindsay nodded. "But she'll come around," she said, wanting to believe it was true.

"It doesn't matter," Heather said.

But of course it did matter, because Suzanne wasn't just Nathan's mom—she was Silver's grandmother.

Obviously the toddler had lots of people in her life who loved her, but the apparent rejection of her existence by family would sting. And even though Silver wasn't aware of the connection or the rejection, Heather was, and Lindsay understood the instinctive need of a mother to protect and soothe her child.

"And anyway, the fewer people who know or acknowledge—the truth, the better. I dealt with enough whispers and snickers when my belly popped out only two months after James and I were married."

"People will talk, if and when the truth of Silver's paternity gets out," Lindsay acknowledged. "And it will be the hottest topic around town for ten minutes, until something newer and hotter comes up, so you shouldn't waste your time worrying about it."

"You're not worried about how that ten minutes of gossip will affect Elliott and Avenlea?"

"Of course I am," she admitted. "But I think they'll accept the truth easier, in the end, if it isn't covered up by a lie."

"That's something to think about," the other woman mused.

"I just want to know that you're not leaving Haven because we came back."

"We're not," Heather said. "We're leaving because this is a great career opportunity for James. They've offered him the position twice before, and if he turns it down this time, it probably won't be offered to him again."

Lindsay nodded. "Then I'll wish you luck in Texas and ask you to keep in touch."

The other woman was obviously surprised by this. "Why would you want me to keep in touch?"

"Because Silver is Elliott and Avenlea's half sister," she said. "And regardless of how you and I might feel about one another, they're family."

Heather nodded slowly as she shifted her gaze to the two little girls, their heads close as they chatted together.

Sisters already on their way to becoming friends.

"There's no need to be nervous," Angela Gilmore said, joining Lindsay at the paddock fence late the following Saturday morning.

"What gave me away?"

"Your white-knuckle grip on the rail."

Lindsay looked down at her hands. Sure enough, the knuckles were white and her fingernails were biting into the wood. She'd hoped to take pictures, to document this milestone moment, but there was no point in taking her phone out of her pocket when she knew she wouldn't be able to hold it steady.

"Mitch won't let her get hurt," Angela assured her.

"I know," she agreed.

And yet, that knowledge did nothing to loosen the knots in her belly.

"But she's a little girl on a big horse," the older woman noted, instinctively understanding the source of Lindsay's apprehension.

Technically Maurice was a pony but, compared to her daughter, he was a beast.

"Mitchell put Elliott on the back of his first pony before he was three, so he insisted that Avenlea should have the same opportunity." Elliott was riding, too, sitting tall in the saddle of Gaston—a second pony that Mitchell had on a lead.

"And look at her," Angela urged. "She has absolutely no fear."

"Sometimes a little fear is healthy," Lindsay noted.

Mitchell's mom chuckled. "I heard about her jumping off the climber at the park."

"She's lucky she didn't need stitches."

And Lindsay was lucky that the amount of blood seemed to have dissuaded her daughter from repeating the action—so far anyway.

"Of course, she'll probably forget all about the park now and want to come out here every day to ride the pony."

"It doesn't seem that many years ago that you were out here almost every day to go riding with Mitchell," Angela noted.

"I know my mom sometimes complained that I spent more time here than at home," Lindsay agreed.

"We were always happy to see you. And while I'm sorry for the circumstances that brought you home again, I'm glad you're home."

"I'm glad to be back," she agreed.

Angela gave her a quick hug.

They watched for several more minutes, Angela chatting away—deliberately distracting Lindsay from worrying about her children.

The "lesson" didn't last long, but both the kids were grinning when Mitchell set them back on solid ground.

Lindsay exhaled a silent sigh of relief as they raced toward her, still wearing their riding helmets.

"Now it's your turn," Angela said to her. "Go saddle up Reba and take a ride with Mitchell."

Lindsay immediately shook her head. "I can't."

"Why not?"

"Because I haven't been on the back of a horse in… years."

"Then you're long overdue. Go on," Mitchell's mom insisted. "I'll keep an eye on Elliott and Avenlea."

But Mitchell was one step ahead, and the mare was already tacked and waiting for her when Elliott and

Avenlea skipped off with Angela, happy to embark on new adventures.

He helped her up in the saddle and encouraged her to walk around the paddock, to get accustomed to the feel of the horse beneath her, while he went to tack his own mount. She signaled the mare to switch from a walk to a trot.

"Looks like it's coming back to you," he noted approvingly, as he led Kenny out of the barn.

"Just like riding a bike," she said. "Except it's riding a horse."

He grinned and effortlessly vaulted into the saddle on the back of the chestnut gelding.

Lindsay, feeling a little more confident now, urged the mare to canter, then tested control by bringing her back down to a trot and a walk again.

"But I have to admit, it feels as if you and your mom conspired against me," she grumbled, as he brought Kenny up alongside Reba.

"I'm not forcing you to go anywhere you don't want to go," he said. "We can stay right here in the paddock, if that's where you're more comfortable."

Though his tone was casual enough, she sensed that there was a deeper meaning to his words—almost as if he was asking about their relationship as much as a trail ride.

She lifted her eyes to meet his. "Open the gate."

He grinned again and did as she instructed.

She let him lead the way, and they headed toward the mountains that rose up in the distance, following the path of Crooked Creek. Fed by the recent snowmelt, the creek, for which the neighboring ranch had been named, gurgled and bubbled over the rocks.

"Hold up," Mitchell said.

She held up, thinking that he'd spotted some kind of hazard that might spook her mount into throwing its rider. "What is it—a snake?"

"Nothing like that," he assured her, as he brought his mount close to hers. Then he tipped his hat back, lowered his head and kissed her, long and slow and deep.

"I'll hold up for one of your kisses anytime," she said, when he finally eased his mouth from hers.

"I couldn't resist," he told her. "You just look so pretty, with your cheeks pink from the wind and your eyes shining bright."

"I forgot how much I loved riding," she admitted. "No doubt I'll regret this outing tomorrow, when every muscle in my body aches, but right now it feels good."

"Yeah, it does," he said, brushing his lips over hers again. "I'm glad you let my mom talk you into it."

"Have you ever tried to say no to your mom?"

"I've tried," he said. "I haven't succeeded."

"Because she's a five-foot four-inch bulldozer," Lindsay said.

He chuckled. "That's a pretty good description—and one that she'd own proudly."

"So…how long do you think we can be gone before she starts to worry—or wonder?" she asked curiously.

"Are you kidding? She's so thrilled to have Elliott and Avenlea to dote on, we could be gone for a week and, when we returned, she'd ask why we came back so soon."

"Well, it's not really fair, you know. All of David Gilmore's adult children are married—or at least engaged—and having babies. Is it too much to ask for at least one of her kids to give her a grandbaby or two to spoil?"

"Sounds like you two had quite a chat," he mused wryly.

"I think she was trying to take my mind off the fact that my not yet three-year-old daughter was riding a pony that weighs twenty times more than Avenlea."

"You know I'd never let her be hurt."

"And that's the only reason she was in that saddle."

She felt her cell phone vibrate inside her pocket. "It's a message from Suzanne," she said, when she'd pulled it out to glance at the screen.

"Is there a problem?"

"A partner from Arthur's old firm is in town and wants to take them out for dinner, so she's asking if we can postpone the sleepover until next week." Lindsay was already texting a reply.

"I guess that means you don't have to rush back to town."

"It also means that I won't be able to come back here tonight," she said, genuinely disappointed.

"I could come to your place," he suggested.

She shook her head. "A tempting offer, but you know Avenlea wakes up several times in the night."

"So we'll reschedule for next week," he said.

"Or…"

"I'm listening."

"If I remember correctly, there's a hunting cabin not too far from here."

"On the other side of the creek," he told her.

Which meant it was on Crooked Creek property.

"That's right," she said, nodding. "It was Brielle who had a sleepover there one time." She smiled. "Which is how I know where the key is."

Mother's Day started early for Lindsay, with a video chat with her mom in Phoenix. The glittery sparkle on Marilyn Delgado's cheek confirmed that she'd received the cards that Elliott and Avenlea had made and Lindsay had sent—along with an electronic gift card for her favorite boutique in their retirement village.

The cards had turned out well, and the kids had seemed to enjoy making them, but Lindsay had already decided that next year she'd give her money to Hallmark and save herself finding glitter everywhere more than two weeks after their card-making session.

After breakfast they stopped by to see Aunt Kristyne, who was celebrating her first ever Mother's Day. They didn't stay long, because it was obvious Gabe had plans to completely spoil the new mom—and because they still had more flowers and glittery cards to deliver to Gramma T.

At the Thomases' house on Miners' Pass, they sat out on the back deck, chatting and enjoying the afternoon sunshine. Elliott and Avenlea, never happy sitting for too long unless there was a screen in front of them, were kicking a ball around in the backyard. When they'd worked up a thirst, Arthur took them into the house to get them a drink.

"And maybe some ice cream," he said with a wink.

It was the perfect opening, Lindsay decided, to talk to her mother-in-law without the kids interrupting.

"I thought you might like to know that Silver comes to story time at nine-thirty on Wednesdays."

"Why would that be of any interest to me?"

"Because she's your granddaughter and you should get to know her."

Suzanne's hand trembled slightly as she lifted her cup of tea, then set it down again without drinking. "I don't understand how you can be so accepting of the... situation."

"I'm never going to be happy that Nate cheated on me," Lindsay said. "But he did, and a beautiful little girl came out of it."

Her mother-in-law was quiet for a long minute before she said, "I heard they're moving to Texas."

Lindsay nodded. "At the end of the summer."

"That's probably for the best. Then you won't have to worry about running into that woman and her daughter every time you run an errand."

"I'm not worried."

"You should be." Suzanne pressed her lips together to hide their quivering. "Because if people knew—or even suspected—that Nathan was the father of that child... they'd say horrible things about my son. Your husband."

"Horrible things such as that he cheated on his pregnant wife with his high school girlfriend and got her pregnant?"

"He made a mistake."

"No." Lindsay shook her head. "He broke his vows. It wasn't an accident—it was a choice."

"I wish he'd never come home for my party," her mother-in-law confided now. "If he'd stayed in Alaska, it never would have happened."

Lindsay had thought the same thing when she first learned of her husband's infidelity. But once she'd taken some time to think about it, she wasn't so sure. In any event, the how and why and even the who didn't matter—what mattered was Silver.

"I know how much it means to you to know that a part of Nathan lives on in his children. Well, a part of him lives on in Silver, too. How can you not want to know her? To love her as much as I know you love Elliott and Avenlea?"

"I know she's a part of him," Suzanne finally admitted, her eyes shiny with unshed tears. "But acknowledging her paternity seems disloyal…to you."

Lindsay's throat tightened with unexpected emotion. "The human heart has an amazing capacity to love," she said gently. "Don't close yours off from the possibility of loving Silver—or letting her love you and Arthur. And I know she will, if you give her a chance."

By the time Lindsay got her kids home later that afternoon, she was ready for a nap. Instead, she had to put fresh sheets on the beds she'd stripped earlier that morning—Avenlea's first, because the little girl was overdue for *her* nap—then deal with the laundry that had piled up throughout the week.

Thankfully, Elliott was content to play with his LEGO bricks while she tackled the chores, and she managed to clean both the upstairs and downstairs bathrooms in between loads of washing.

Oh, the glamorous life of a single mom, she thought, as she walked out of the laundry room with a basket of clean clothes on her hip.

"I'm hungry," Elliott said, when she peeked in the family room to check on him.

Avenlea, now up from her nap, echoed the sentiment. "I hun-wee, too."

"Me, three," Lindsay said.

Her son wasn't amused. "What's for supper?"

Which was when she realized that in all the planning she'd done for the day, she hadn't given a single thought to dinner.

"I'll take a look in the freezer to see if we've got any chicken fingers," she decided. Though she preferred to make her own chicken strips, she tried to keep a box of the frozen variety in the freezer for occasions such as this.

"Yay!" Avenlea said, proving that they were indeed a go-to kid-pleaser.

Unfortunately, there were only three chicken fingers—and a whole bunch of crumbs—left in the box.

"How about cheese strings and olives?" she suggested, thinking of the appetizer plate Mitchell had managed to put together on New Year's Eve despite her fridge being mostly empty.

"Olives?" Elliott made a face. "Yuck."

"Yuck," Avenlea echoed, conveniently forgetting

that she gobbled them like candy whenever Lindsay put them on the table.

"Okay, let's figure out a Plan C," she said, moving things around in the freezer in the hope that she might find one of her mom's neatly labeled containers hidden at the back.

"Doorbell!" Elliott shouted, in case she hadn't heard it.

"Don't open—"

"It's Uncle Mitch!" he called out.

"Uncamitch!" Avenlea echoed.

"He's got pizza!"

"An' fwo-wuhs!"

Lindsay closed the freezer and went to the door to greet her friend (with some far-too-infrequent but spectacular benefits).

"Happy Mother's Day," he said, offering her a bouquet of orange lilies, yellow gerberas and red carnations with spikes of purple Veronica flowers and pennycress.

"Oh, Mitchell—they're beautiful." She kissed his cheek—the only display of affection she would allow herself in front of her children.

He slid his arm around her, to give her a friendly hug, but let his hand slide over the curve of her butt as she moved away.

She sent him a warning look; he grinned, unrepentant.

"Thank you for the flowers. And the pizza."

"I didn't want you to have to cook today."

An incredibly thoughtful gesture, but it was his company that really made her happy. She hadn't expected to see him today, assuming that he'd be spending the day celebrating his own mother.

While she filled a vase with water for her flowers, Mitchell got out plates and napkins. They moved easily around one another—and Elliott and Avenlea—in the kitchen, almost as if they were a family.

And maybe they could be, someday. But now, she was trying to enjoy the moments they had together and not think too far ahead.

After everyone had their fill of pizza, Lindsay started to push away from the table, but Mitchell asked her to stay put. He whispered first in Elliott's ear, then in Avenlea's, and her children scampered away.

"Are you conspiring again?" she asked suspiciously.

"It's not a conspiracy, it's a surprise," he said, as the kids came back to the table.

He nodded to Avenlea, who brought her hands out from behind her back to give her mom an oversize envelope. Inside was an oversize card, obviously home-made but thankfully not covered in glitter.

The front cover read: "Happy Mother's Day to the best mom…" And when she opened it up, the sentiment finished inside with, "Hands down!"

And around the words were their handprints, labeled and dated for posterity.

"Oh." She blinked away the tears that filled her eyes again and looked at Mitchell questioningly. "Did *you* do this?"

He shook his head. "I wish I could take the credit, but no, it was my mom. The day you brought the kids out to the Circle G. Actually, it was Olivia's idea—something they do as an art project at school."

"Thank you," she said, opening her arms to draw her son and daughter in for a family hug.

"There's something else, too," Elliott said, wriggling free of her grasp to give her a small square box neatly wrapped in silver paper with a tiny gold bow.

She recognized the trademark wrapping of The Gold Mine—a local jewelry store. She turned the box over and slid a fingernail beneath the seam, breaking the tape.

"Just tear the paper," Mitchell urged.

"It's too pretty to tear," she protested.

"Is she this careful on Christmas morning?" he asked Elliott.

The little boy nodded, rolling his eyes.

"It takes forever and ever."

"Forever? I think I'd have to see it to believe it."

She wanted to say that maybe this year he would, but she wasn't sure if they were at the stage in their relationship where they should be planning more than seven months into the future. Instead, she focused on unwrapping her present, then opening the hinged lid of the gray velvet box.

Inside was a delicate gold chain with a heart-shaped pendant inscribed with the word "Mommy" in cursive script.

"This is—" she had to pause to clear her throat "—really beautiful."

"Turn it over," Mitchell suggested.

She turned the heart over to see that Elliott and Avenlea's birth dates had been engraved on the reverse.

"You like it?" Elliott asked.

"It is the best Mother's Day present ever," she said, drawing both her kids close for another hug—and kisses this time.

And then, because she couldn't resist, she kissed Mitchell, too.

The next weekend was Avenlea's third birthday.

Lindsay had invited several of her daughter's friends from day care to the party. Of course it was a princess-themed party, with pink and purple streamers and balloons, silver crowns for the guests to decorate, and a pin-the-tiara-on-the-princess game. Of course, when "Unca Mitch's" surprise bouncy castle was delivered, a few of the neighborhood children excitedly crashed the party, too. (Wanting to prove that she was a big girl now that she was three, Avenlea was trying hard to enunciate her words more clearly.)

There were crown-shaped peanut butter and jelly sandwiches (she'd checked to make sure none of the guests had a nut allergy), fruit wands and sparkling raspberry lemonade, and vanilla cupcakes with pink icing or chocolate cupcakes with purple icing for dessert.

The party was scheduled to last ninety minutes—long enough for the guests to decorate their crowns, play some games, and have something to eat and drink, and short enough that they'd be on their way home before they started getting bored or cranky, as three year olds tended to do. Pickup time was noted on the invitation as two o'clock; it was now almost four and Lindsay had only just sent the last birthday guest home with her princess-themed loot bag.

"I thought you said this was going to be a low-key party," Kristyne commented, as she settled at the kitchen table to nurse her baby.

"That was the plan," Lindsay agreed, ignoring the twinge she felt as she watched Harper suckle at her mother's breast. She began to pack up the leftovers.

She'd still been nursing Avenlea when Nathan was killed, but the upheaval and stress had forced her to switch her infant daughter to a bottle much sooner than she'd intended. Not that Avenlea seemed to have suffered in any way because of it, but Lindsay couldn't help feeling as if they'd both been shortchanged as a result of the abrupt weaning. Of course, the loss of the little girl's father was a much bigger struggle, and when Lindsay had said her final goodbye to her husband, she'd been certain she was saying goodbye to any hope of expanding her family.

She and Mitch hadn't talked about what the future might hold for them—they were nowhere near that stage in their relationship. But a tiny hope had begun to resurrect itself within her.

"Do you need me to tell you that a bouncy castle is not low-key?" Kristyne asked her now. "No wonder all the neighborhood kids were here."

"The bouncy castle was Mitchell's doing." She looked out the window over the sink that gave her a prime view of the backyard, where Mitchell and Gabe were jumping inside the inflatable playhouse with Elliott and Avenlea. Just like little kids.

"And the smile on your face… I'm guessing that's Mitchell's doing, too?" her sister said, sounding amused.

Lindsay didn't even try to deny it. "Yeah."

"It's been a long time since I've seen you smile like that," Kristyne noted. "It makes me happy to see you happy."

"I am happy," she said, as she continued to wrap up the leftover food. "Sometimes I worry that I don't have any right to be so happy."

"Why would you say that?" her sister demanded.

"Because Nathan's gone and—"

"Stop right there," Kristyne interjected. "How can you think you owe him any loyalty—more than two years after his death—when he didn't offer you the same while he was alive?"

"It's not about loyalty," Lindsay denied. "At least, I don't think so. It's just that he was my first love…and I really thought it would last forever."

It felt silly to admit it aloud, especially to her sister, who, though two years younger, had a lot more experience with romantic relationships.

"Nathan wasn't your first love," Kristyne said confidently. "He might have been your first lover, but you loved Mitchell first."

"That was nothing more than a childhood crush."

"And now?" her sister prompted.

"And now…" her gaze shifted to the window again "…we're taking things one day at a time."

"So you haven't talked about getting married and having a couple more kids?" Kristyne, always attuned to her sister's thoughts and feelings, pressed.

"No." Lindsay's response was immediate and adamant.

"Why not?" Kristyne eased her nipple from her daughter's mouth and shifted the baby to the other breast to continue feeding. "If I'd had any doubts before today, watching Mitchell with all those kids proved he'd be a great father."

Lindsay had watched him, too. And watching him, her heart had yearned.

"And did you see him with Harper?" her sister asked.

"I saw the panicked look on his face when you shoved your baby into his arms."

"I had to go to the bathroom, Gabe wasn't in the immediate vicinity and my bladder control isn't what it used to be," Kristyne said in her defense. "But by the time I came back, Mitchell had Harper tucked in the crook of his arm and was cooing to her like a pro."

"Yeah, I saw that, too," Lindsay confided.

"You always said you wanted four kids."

"One day at a time," she reminded her sister.

"Hmm," Kristyne said. "Are you worried that the Thomases will disapprove of your relationship with Mitchell?"

"No," she said. Truthfully, she hadn't given any thought to how Nathan's parents might react when they found out that she was in a relationship with someone new—until today, at the party, when Mitchell leaned close to say something to her and she caught Suzanne frowning in their direction.

"Because I noticed that they didn't hang around for very long this afternoon," her sister continued.

"They were on their way to Elko, to meet friends for dinner."

"I guess that would explain why they were overdressed for a backyard party." Kristyne lifted the now-sleeping infant to her shoulder and gently rubbed her back.

"I can do that part," Lindsay said, reaching for the baby.

Her sister relinquished her daughter willingly so that she could more easily refasten the cups of her nursing bra.

As Kristyne was adjusting her top, Lindsay heard her computer ringing in the den.

"Mom and Dad said they were going to Skype at four thirty," she said, suddenly remembering.

"You answer that—I'll get the birthday girl," Kristyne said.

Within minutes, everyone was gathered around the computer to join in the conversation. Of course, Avenlea was front and center, leaning close to the camera to ensure Gramma and Grampa D could see her as she regaled them with details of her party.

"An' we jumped in the bouncy castle an' had cupcakes an' pwesents."

"You had a bouncy castle?" Though Marilyn was talking to her granddaughter, she looked at the birthday girl's mom quizzically.

"Courtesy of Uncle Mitch," Lindsay explained, with a pointed glance at the man in question.

He just shrugged and grinned.

"An' I gots wots an' wots of pwesents," Avenlea announced. "Even Hawpuh bwin'd me a pwesent."

"Brought," Lindsay automatically corrected her daughter.

"A Bitty Baby Doll," Avenlea continued. "And Auntie Kwisty ate Hawpuh's cupcake *an'* hew own cupcake."

"Tattletale," Kristyne muttered from the background.

"She ate mine, too," Gabe piped up.

"They were minicupcakes," his wife muttered. "And the doctor said that I need an extra four to five hundred calories while I'm nursing."

"I don't think she meant four to five hundred cupcake calories," her husband said.

"But don' wo-wy," Avenlea continued talking to her grandparents. "Mommy saved cupcakes for you. She put 'em in the fwee-zuh so Auntie Kwisty couldn't find 'em."

"But now I know where to look," Kristyne said, grinning.

Avenlea clapped a hand over her mouth.

"I think it's a little late for that," Lindsay told her daughter.

Marilyn and Jackson exchanged amused glances. "Well, that was very thoughtful. Thank you, Lindsay. And we're sorry we couldn't be there for your party, Avenlea, but we're happy to know you had a good birthday."

"'S'okay," the birthday girl said. "Weast you sended a pwesent."

"Avenlea," Lindsay admonished, heat rising in her cheeks. "It's about the *thought*, not the *present*."

"Well, I'm gwad Gwamma an' Gwampa *fought* to send a pwesent," Avenlea said, making everyone laugh.

Chapter Sixteen

"I think I'd rather wrangle cattle than chase after kids all day," Mitch said. "I'm exhausted."

"It was a busy day," Lindsay acknowledged, dropping onto the sofa beside him and letting her head tip back against his shoulder. "But a really good one."

"All the kids seemed to have fun."

"Mmm-hmm," she agreed. "I just wish Silver had come to the party."

"You invited Heather's daughter?" He didn't know why he was surprised—it was exactly the kind of thing Lindsay would do.

She nodded. "Heather RSVP'd her regrets, but I was hoping she'd change her mind."

"It might have been interesting if she'd shown up when Arthur and Suzanne were here. Avenlea's party would have been the talk of the town—a bouncy castle *and* fireworks."

"Or you would have been disappointed by the lack of fireworks," she said. "Because there weren't any when Arthur came into the library last week while Silver was there for story time."

"I'm guessing the timing of his visit wasn't a coincidence?"

Now she shook her head. "He wanted to meet his youngest granddaughter."

"How did that go?"

"I wasn't privy to their conversation, but I think it went well," she said. "I saw him talking to Heather while Silver played at the train table with a couple other kids, and though they left a short while later, Arthur stopped at the desk first to thank me."

"Suzanne wasn't there?"

"No, but I have no doubt he'll bring her around."

"Whatever Suzanne knew or suspected three years ago, it seems safe to assume that she didn't share it with her husband," he noted.

"I'd agree. As smart as my father-in-law is when it comes to legal matters, he's remarkably oblivious to the world around him."

"It was good to see him today," Mitch said. "And Suzanne."

"It was good of you to give up your Saturday to help with the birthday party."

"I had fun, too," he said.

"You did look like you were having fun," she

acknowledged. "Especially when you took off your boots and joined the kids in the bouncy castle."

He grinned. "Yeah, it was worth every penny."

She shook her head, but he could tell that she was fighting against the smile tugging at the corners of her mouth.

"Do you know what I was thinking tonight—when you were helping get Elliott and Avenlea ready for bed?" she asked.

"'Will these kids please go to sleep so that I can get this man naked'?" he guessed.

She lost the battle against the smile. "Aside from that, I was thinking about how easy you are with the kids, how good you are at all the family stuff."

"You have great kids," he said.

"And I was wondering," she continued, determined to finish her thought, "why you never got married and had a bunch of kids of your own."

"I'm only thirty-four years old," he reminded her. "Maybe you shouldn't write me off just yet."

"You're thirty-four years old and you haven't, as far as I know, ever had a relationship that lasted longer than two years. And your most recent only lasted six months."

"Are you worried that our relationship might have an expiration date?" he asked her.

"No. Maybe."

"Well, don't," he told her. "There's one very specific reason that none of those other relationships worked out—because I was already in love with you."

* * *

He hadn't meant to tell her just yet. And not when they were casually sprawled on her sofa at the end of a long day. That was his mistake.

And though he'd known they were at different stages in their relationship, he hadn't anticipated that she'd be surprised to learn the truth of his feelings for her. But maybe he should have, because he'd been in love with her for half his life and she was still trying to wrap her head around the fact that she was in an intimate relationship with someone other than the man she'd married.

So he'd asked her not to say anything, inwardly cringing as he imagined the various ways she might respond.

You have to know how much I care about you.

You're one of my best friends in the world—of course I love you, too.

And he really didn't want to hear either of those sentiments.

So he'd kissed her goodbye and left before he pushed her for more than she was ready to give.

For weeks—okay, months—he'd been reminding himself to be patient. To remember that he'd loved her a lot longer than she'd loved him. Because although she hadn't said the words back to him that night, he had to believe that she loved him, too.

But she'd been through a lot in the past few years. Not just the sudden and unexpected death of her husband, but the more recent discovery of his infidelity and the existence of another child. She was smart to be cautious, to take some time, to be sure.

And while she was taking her time, he would be there for her, as he'd always been there for her. Showing her how good they were together—not just him and Lindsay, but Elliott and Avenlea, too. A family.

So the following Saturday, he showed up at her door again, not to put any pressure on her but hopefully persuade her to bring the kids out to the Circle G to go riding again. Then they could barbecue some steaks— he'd cut up steak bites for Elliott and Avenlea to dip in ketchup—and just enjoy a beautiful day together.

His easy smile slipped when Suzanne Thomas answered the door and he realized that he'd been so preoccupied with making plans for the day, he hadn't noticed that the vehicle in the driveway didn't belong to Lindsay but to her mother-in-law.

After his friend's passing, Mitch had occasionally gone into town to check in on Suzanne and Arthur, and he knew they'd appreciated his efforts. But since he'd confronted Suzanne about Nathan's affair, he'd received a much chillier reception whenever their paths crossed. While Arthur seemed to be of the opinion that what was done was done, Suzanne appeared to blame him for forcing her to acknowledge her son's infidelity.

"Hello, Mrs. Thomas," he said.

"Mitchell." She inclined her head slightly. "Lindsay didn't mention that you would be stopping by."

"She didn't know," he said. "I had some things to do in town and thought I'd take a chance that she'd be home."

"Well, she's not," Suzanne said.

Her polite but cool response was almost drowned out by Avenlea shouting: "Unca Mitch! Unca Mitch!"

He scooped her up in his arms; she planted a smacking kiss on his cheek.

"Are you gonna have wunch wif us? Gwamma's makin' mac an' cheese not fwom a box!"

"Mac and cheese not from a box?" he echoed incredulously. "I didn't know there was any such thing."

Which was a great big fib, because his mom had always made it from scratch, too. But there were admittedly a couple of the trademark blue boxes in his pantry at the Circle G.

"Can you stay?" Avenlea asked. "P'ease?"

Suzanne didn't object to the invitation, but she didn't say anything to indicate that he would be welcome to join them, either. But that was okay—he had no desire to prolong this awkward encounter with her.

"Sorry, princess. I've got some errands to run."

"I wun ew-ans wif you?"

"Not today," he said.

"'Mo-wow?" she asked hopefully.

He had to smile. "I'll let you know. Okay?"

"'Kay," she agreed, bending over his arm to indicate that she wanted down.

He set her back on the floor and she raced off again, returning to whatever she'd been doing when she heard him at the door.

Suzanne, who'd watched the interaction with thinly veiled disapproval, seemed eager now to send him on his way. "When Lindsay gets home from Sunset Vista, I'll be sure to tell her that you stopped by."

The mention of Sunset Vista was clearly to make a point—and not at all subtle.

Mitch knew that Lindsay visited the memorial gardens regularly if not frequently—usually on Nathan's birthday, their anniversary and the anniversary of his death. Today wasn't any of those days. But he pushed his questions about the visit aside in the interest of making peace with Suzanne, because he knew it was important for his future with Lindsay that he get along with her in-laws, who would always be part of her life.

"Nate was my friend, too," he reminded her.

"But you didn't let that stop you from taking up with his wife, did you?"

He didn't know how she knew about the change in his relationship with Lindsay—or even if she did. Perhaps she was just fishing for information. Either way, he wasn't going to lie to her.

"His widow," he corrected, meeting her gaze steadily. "Who honored the vows she made to her husband every single day of the five and a half years they were married."

Suzanne looked away first. "Because she loved him."

An undeniable fact that Mitch had accepted long ago. But Nathan was her past, and he wanted to be her future—if Lindsay would let him.

"But he's gone now," he said gently. "And if Lindsay's finally ready to move on with her life with someone else, would that be so bad? Shouldn't she have a chance to be happy again?

"Wouldn't it be nice for Elliott and Avenlea to have someone in their lives? Not to take the place of their dad, but maybe fill a little bit of the hole left by his absence?

"Shouldn't you, as their grandmother, want that for them? Or are you afraid that if Lindsay moves on, she'll cut you out of your grandchildren's lives? And if you are, then you don't know her at all."

"Of course I want what's best for Lindsay and Elliott and Avenlea," she said. "I just don't think she's as committed to you as you are to her."

"I guess that's something for me and her to figure out."

"Has she told you that she loves you?" Suzanne asked.

It was a shot in the dark—there was no way she could know what he and Lindsay had talked about. But something in his expression must have confirmed that the words hit their target, because she took aim again.

"She hasn't, has she? Because she's still in love with Nathan."

Mitch didn't want to believe it, but maybe it was true.

And if it was true, maybe it was time for him to cut his losses and move on—even if it meant cutting his own heart out in the process.

Lindsay took her time strolling through the gardens, basking in the sunshine and breathing in the scents of fresh-cut grass and spring flowers. She looked around, for the first time truly seeing and appreciating the neatly manicured lawns, trees with discreet plaques, benches dedicated in memory of loved ones who'd passed.

She and Nathan had never seriously talked about

what arrangements should be made in case of an untimely death. A common oversight on the part of young couples, or so she'd been told after the fact. But she did remember a comment he'd made when they'd attended a funeral together for one of his distant relatives. As they'd stood by the graveside, listening to the minister say a last prayer, he'd told her that he never wanted to be buried in the ground. *"Cremate me and scatter my ashes."*

Her memory of that expressed wish had led to direct conflict with Arthur and Suzanne, who insisted that their son should be immortalized with an ornate marker carved of glossy marble. In the end, they'd compromised on cremation with some of the ashes scattered and the rest interred here, so that Avenlea and Elliott would have a place to go where they might feel connected to their dad. Lindsay had been pretty sure it was Suzanne who wanted to feel connected, but today she was equally glad there was a place to go, to say goodbye.

She hadn't brought flowers, because she knew that Suzanne had made arrangements for regular deliveries. This week it was yellow daffodils. As she looked at Nathan's name and the dates of his life etched in the stone facade of the niche, beside the sunny blossoms, she couldn't help but mourn a life cut so tragically short.

"You might be wondering why I'm here today," she said. "Or maybe you know. Either way, I've spent a lot of time trying to sort through my feelings about a lot of things lately, and I wanted to share them with you.

"Losing you absolutely devastated me, but I was finally starting to come to terms with the fact that you were gone, finally able to appreciate the memories of our years together and the beautiful children we had together.

"And then, finding out that you'd cheated on me... it was almost like losing you again. Because that discovery took away a part of us, forcing me to accept that what I knew and believed about our relationship wasn't true."

She'd been hurt and angry, not just because of what he'd done, but because her discovery of his actions had taken away the one thing she had left—her memories of *them*. Making her grieve all over again for the loss of what they'd had and leaving her with more questions than answers.

But then, a few days later when she was tucking Elliott and Avenlea into their beds, she realized that the why—and even the how many—didn't really matter. Because it was over and done and nothing in the past could be changed.

So she'd forgiven him, because holding on to her hurt and anger wasn't doing her any good. Because she needed to let go in order to move on.

And she was finally ready to move on.

"One of the strangest parts of all this is that I've gotten to know Heather a lot better than I ever did in high school. And I've gotten to know her daughter—*your daughter*—too. I don't know what would have happened between us if you'd found out that she was pregnant before that last trip, but I do wish you'd had the chance to know Silver. She looks a little bit like each of Elliott and Avenlea, but she's one hundred percent her own person, and I know you would have loved her as much as you loved our children."

Lindsay lifted a hand to brush an errant tear from her lashes. "I won't ever let Elliott and Avenlea forget you, but it's time to let someone else into our lives to complete our family. Maybe you know I'm talking about Mitchell. And maybe you saw that one coming. Apparently I'm the only one who was surprised to learn that he'd had feelings for me for a long time—and even more surprised to discover the depth of my feelings for him.

"I'm not asking for your permission or blessing. I just wanted you to know that I'm moving on. I will always love you and be grateful to you for the two amazing children we had together, but I'm ready to love someone else now, to trust and hope in the future again."

She didn't know what she expected to feel at the end of her monologue, but when she finished saying what she needed to say, she felt better. Not just unburdened but optimistic. Excited about and looking forward to her future with Mitchell—and eager to tell him so.

Except that Mitchell wasn't home when she got to the Circle G. His truck was in the driveway, but when she knocked, it was MG who answered the door.

"You might want to check the barn," he suggested, in response to her query about his brother. "He said something about going for a ride."

So she checked the barn, but he wasn't there, either—and neither was Kenny, confirming MG's suspicion that Mitchell was out on horseback. Which left her with two options: saddle up one of the other horses and try to track him down or wait for him to return.

Waiting obviously made the most sense, but Lindsay felt as if she'd been waiting for this moment long enough and she didn't want to wait any longer.

She was contemplating her next move when Olivia exited a stall at the far end of the barn with Reba.

"He's not here," Mitchell's sister said, dispensing with the usual pleasantries.

Lindsay nodded. "Do you think it would be okay if I saddled up one of your horses and went after him?"

"That depends on what you plan on saying when you find him."

"Isn't that between your brother and me?"

"Not if I'm the one who has to mop up the blood pouring out of his broken heart."

"I would never do anything to hurt Mitchell."

"Then why did he look crushed when he got back from your place?" Olivia challenged, starting to pass.

"Wait." Lindsay stepped in front of her, blocking her path. "When was Mitchell at my place?"

Now his sister frowned. "Earlier today."

"I haven't seen him since Thursday." But if what Olivia was saying was true, if he'd stopped by her place… She winced. "Suzanne's watching the kids for me today."

The other woman studied her for a long moment while she considered this explanation, then finally handed Reba's reins to her. "I've got other things I should be doing anyway."

"Are you going to give me any hint as to which direction he might have headed?" she asked, as Mitchell's sister walked away.

"North."

It was a vague and rather unhelpful response, but after Lindsay had mounted the horse and turned to face north, she realized it was the same direction Mitchell had always taken whenever they went riding together. Nudging the mare into action, she followed the familiar route, silently praying that it was the right one.

Twenty minutes later, she found him by the stand of trees where they used to hang out when they were younger. He was reclined on the ground, his back against the trunk of one of the trees, with a small note-book and a pen in hand. Kenny was nearby, grazing.

He rose to his feet as she drew nearer, tucking the book and pen in his back pocket.

"Hey," he said cautiously.

Lindsay smiled. "Hey."

He helped her dismount—because riding a horse wasn't quite as easy as riding a bike—and then tapped Reba's flank, giving the mare permission to graze with Kenny.

"Did I know you were coming out to the ranch today?" he asked.

"I didn't know until I was on my way here," she said. "But I wanted to tell you that I've been thinking about what you said, last week, and—"

"It's okay," he interrupted. "You don't have to say it. I understand."

She blinked, startled by the abruptness of his tone as much as the interruption. "What do you understand?"

"That you're not ready for a relationship."

She folded her arms over her chest then and huffed out a breath. "You're doing it again."

He frowned. "Doing what?"

"Telling me how I feel, what I want."

"I'm just trying to make this easier on both of us," he told her. "And honestly, it's just as well, because I'm tired of coming in second place to a dead guy."

"Is that really how you feel?"

"It's what it is. And maybe it's partly my own fault, for waiting too long to tell you how I felt. Because I loved you then and I love you now, but I can't do this anymore."

She shook her head. "Well, you're wrong." she said. "About all of it. I *am* ready for a relationship—with *you*."

"Is that what you came out here to say?"

"Actually, what I came out here to say is that I love you, too."

He swallowed. "You do?"

"Why do you sound so surprised?"

"Because you went to the cemetery today."

"You jumped to all kinds of crazy conclusions because I needed to set some things straight with my late husband?" she asked incredulously.

He looked chagrined. "In my defense, I didn't really jump so much as I was pushed."

"Suzanne," she realized.

"I shouldn't have let her get into my head," he admitted. "But everything was always a competition with

Nate, and he never let me forget whenever he came first—like he did with you."

"But I did love you first, even if it was only with the innocent heart of a young girl," she said. "More important, I love you now and I'll love you forever."

"I love you, too," he said, drawing her into his arms.

"And yet you were going to let me walk away," she said accusingly.

"Only because I thought it was what you wanted, and because all I've ever wanted is for you to be happy."

"If you really want me to be happy, you'll hold on to me and never let me go," she said.

"I can do that," he promised.

She lifted her arms to link her hands behind his head. "Are you going to kiss me now?"

"Since when do you wait for me to make the first move?" he teased.

"Good point," she said, and pulled his mouth down to hers.

Epilogue

Three weeks later

Once every five weeks, Lindsay had to work a Saturday afternoon shift at the library. Since she was working today, Mitch decided it was the perfect time for him
to set his plan in motion. A carefully woven plan that
started to unravel as soon as he got back from his shopping excursion with Elliott and Avenlea—and hadn't
that been an adventure?—and discovered Lindsay's
SUV in the driveway despite the fact that it was only
three o'clock and she was scheduled to work until four.

"Where have you guys been?" she asked, when they
walked through the door.

"Mommy! Mommy!" The little girl was across the

room before he could stop her. "Unca Mitch took us shoppin' an' I got a—"

"Secret," Mitch interjected loudly.

"Whoopsie!" She giggled. "So-wee."

"I told you she can't keep a secret," Elliott said, shaking his head with all the exasperation a big brother could muster.

"But she promised that she would," Mitchell said pointedly to Avenlea.

She nodded solemnly. "I pwomise."

Lindsay watched the exchange with amusement. "What's the secret?"

"We're gonna get—"

"In trouble if you give away the secret," Mitch cut her off again.

She clapped a hand over her mouth.

He sighed, shaking his head. "Two minutes," he said. "We haven't been in the house two minutes."

"I told you," Elliott said again.

Mitch turned to Lindsay then with the look of stern disapproval that he'd been practicing on the kids. "I can't believe you were trying to get your three-year-old daughter to spill a secret."

She shrugged, unapologetic. "It was worth a shot."

"What are you doing home already?" he asked instead.

"The power was out at the community center, so the library closed early."

"Obviously circumstances are conspiring against me," he muttered.

"Do you want me to leave?" she asked, sounding amused.

He shook his head. "No. This isn't quite how I'd envisioned doing this, but since I can't count on Avenlea to keep the secret for another two minutes, we're going to improvise."

"What's *improvise* mean?" Elliott asked.

"It means working with what you've got," Mitch explained. "Which is a little girl bursting at the seams, so go ahead, Avenlea, and tell your mom the secret."

"We wanna get may-weed!" she announced, bouncing up and down with excitement.

It took Lindsay a second to translate her daughter's "may-weed" to "married," and then her heart leaped and lodged in her throat.

"Who wants to get married?" she asked cautiously.

"We do," Elliott said. "All of us. So Uncle Mitch can live here and we can be a real family."

She looked at Mitchell then, and saw that he'd dropped down to one knee and was opening a jeweler's box, inside of which was—

Oh.

She laughed, even as her eyes filled with tears that blurred her view of the purple plastic flower ring nestled against the velvet lining.

"I can't believe it," she said. "Where did you find one exactly the same?"

"It's not exactly the same. It's the actual ring I gave you twenty-three years ago."

"But…how?"

He shrugged. "It was either sheer luck or destiny that

I happened to glance down one day as I was leaving and spotted something purple peeking through the snow."

"Avenlea must have dropped it when we left the house that day."

"I so-wee, Mommy," the little girl chimed in now.

Lindsay brushed a hand over her daughter's hair. "It's okay," she said. "Because Uncle Mitch found it."

"I told you it would turn up," he reminded her.

"My first engagement ring," she said, her lips curving. "Given to me by the first boy I ever loved."

"Do you remember what you said when I asked you to marry me that day?" Mitchell asked her.

Her smile widened. "I said that if I had to get married, it might as well be to someone I liked."

"Do you still like me?"

"Yes." She held his gaze for a long moment. "I like you a lot."

"Enough to marry me?" he asked hopefully.

"Yes," she said again, and nodded. "Definitely yes."

He took the ring out of the box now and slid it onto the tip of her third finger—because the band was too small for it to go any farther.

"Obviously I didn't think this through," he said.

"Maybe they could resize it at The Gold Mine," she suggested teasingly.

"Or you could put that one back in your jewelry box for safekeeping and wear this one instead."

This time, the ring he offered was a diamond. Actually, a lot of diamonds, arranged in the shape of a flower.

"It's a little unconventional for an engagement

ring," he acknowledged. "I wanted to stick with the flower theme—but the jeweler promised that you could exchange it for something else, if you want."

"It's unconventional," she agreed. "And absolutely perfect."

He brushed a quick kiss over her lips, but she knew there would be more kisses—and more other stuff—to celebrate later.

"I gots a fwo-wuh, too," Avenlea told her mom now, lifting the delicate silver chain that was around her throat to show off a daisy-shaped pendant with a tiny sparkling stone at its center. "Unca Mitch said it's a pwomise that he's gonna be wif us fo-evuh."

"I got a Marc-André Fleury rookie card," Elliott said with a grin.

"His nickname is 'Flower,'" Mitchell explained.

Because of course he'd figured out a way to let both her children know that his proposal was about them, too. That he didn't just want to marry their mom, he wanted them all to be a family.

"So everyone came home from your shopping trip happy," she said to Mitchell. "But what did you get?"

He pulled Lindsay and Elliott and Avenlea in for a family hug. "Everything I've always wanted."

* * * * *

Look for Kyle and Erin's story,
the next installment in Brenda Harlen's
Match Made in Haven miniseries.
Coming soon to Harlequin Special Edition!

WE HOPE YOU ENJOYED
THIS BOOK FROM

SPECIAL
EDITION

Believe in love. Overcome obstacles. Find happiness.

Relate to finding comfort and strength in the
support of loved ones and enjoy the journey
no matter what life throws your way.

6 NEW BOOKS AVAILABLE EVERY MONTH!

COMING NEXT MONTH FROM

⊞ HARLEQUIN
SPECIAL EDITION

YOU CAN FIND MORE INFORMATION ON UPCOMING HARLEQUIN TITLES, FREE EXCERPTS AND MORE AT HARLEQUIN.COM.

HSECNM0421

Nissa Lang knows Desmond Stilling is out of her league. He's a CEO, she's a teacher. He's gorgeous, she's... not. So when her house-sitting gig falls through and Desmond offers her a place to stay for the summer, she vows not to reveal how she's felt about him since their first—and only—kiss.

Read on for a sneak peek at
Before Summer Ends,
by #1 New York Times *bestselling author*
Susan Mallery.

"You're welcome to join me if you'd like. Unless you have plans. It's Saturday, after all."

Plans as in a date? Yeah, not so much these days. In fact, she hadn't been in a serious relationship since she and James had broken up over two years ago.

"I don't date," she blurted before she could stop herself. "I mean, I can, but I don't. Or I haven't been. Um, lately."

She consciously pressed her lips together to stop herself from babbling like an idiot, despite the fact that the damage was done.

"So, dinner?" Desmond asked, rescuing her without commenting on her babbling.